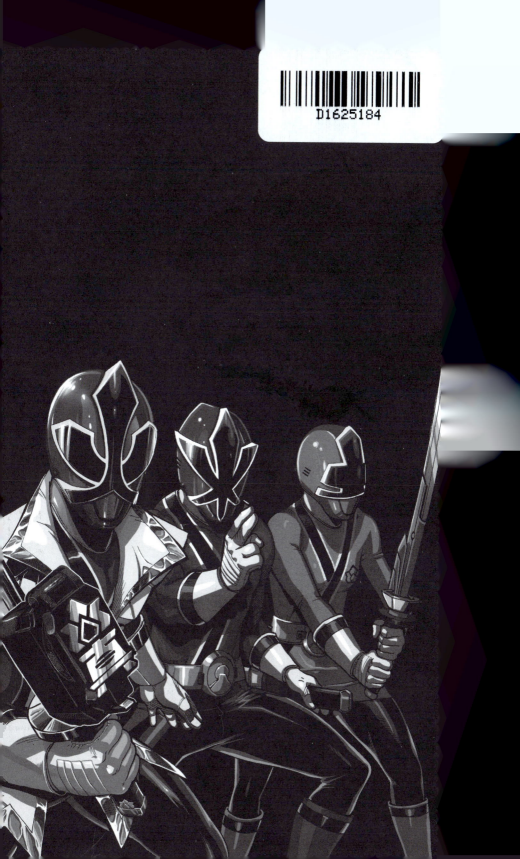

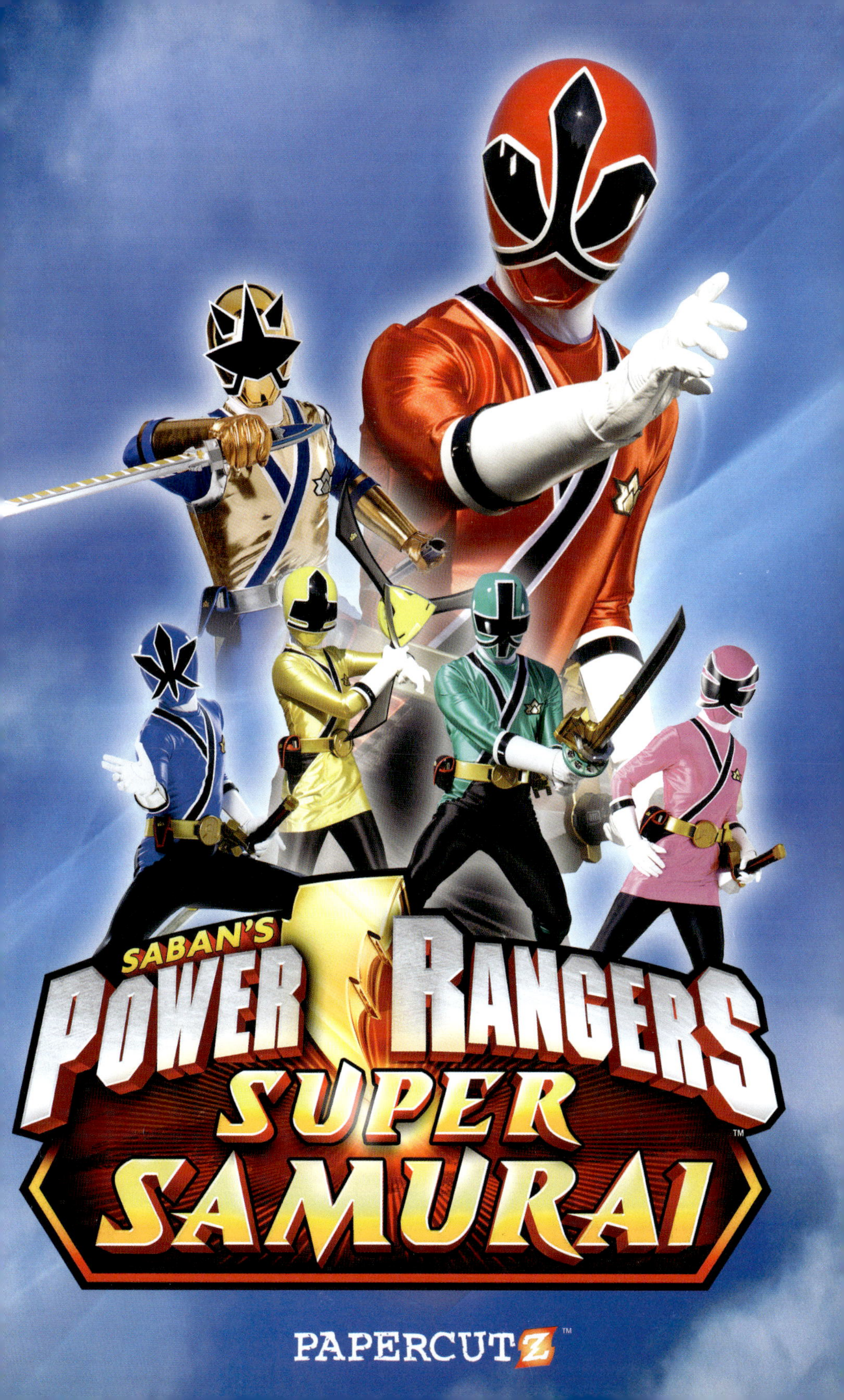
SABAN'S
POWER RANGERS
SUPER SAMURAI
PAPERCUTZ

SABAN'S POWER RANGERS SUPER SAMURAI

Graphic Novels Available From PAPERCUTZ

1 "MEMORY SHORT"
SABAN'S POWER RANGERS SUPER SAMURAI
Stefan Petrucha
Paulo Henrique
PAPERCUTZ

Graphic Novel #1

2 "TERRIBLE TOYS"
Stefan Petrucha • Paulo Henrique
SABAN'S POWER RANGERS SUPER SAMURAI
PAPERCUTZ

Graphic Novel #2

POWER RANGERS graphic novels are available for $6.99 each in paperback, and $10.99 in hardcover. Available from booksellers everywhere. You can also order online from www.papercutz.com. Or call 1-800-886-1223, Monday through Fridays, 9 – 5 EST. MC, Visa, and AmEx accepted. To order by mail, please add $4.00 for postage and handling for first book ordered, $1.00 for each additional book and make check payable to NBM Publishing. Send to: Papercutz, 160 Broadway, Suite 700, East Wing, New York, NY 100038.

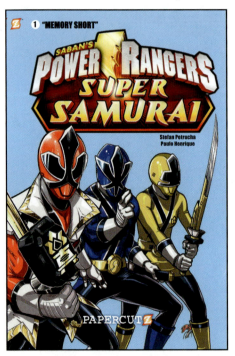

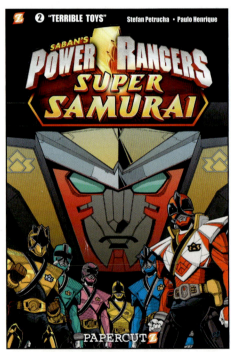

② "TERRIBLE TOYS"

Stefan Petrucha – Writer
Paulo Henrique – Artist
Laurie E. Smith – Colorist

New York

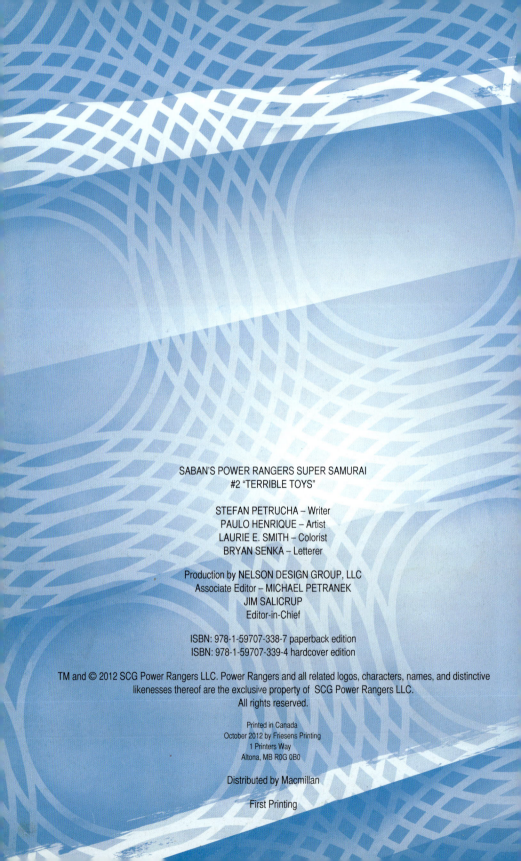

SABAN'S POWER RANGERS SUPER SAMURAI
#2 "TERRIBLE TOYS"

STEFAN PETRUCHA – Writer
PAULO HENRIQUE – Artist
LAURIE E. SMITH – Colorist
BRYAN SENKA – Letterer

Production by NELSON DESIGN GROUP, LLC
Associate Editor – MICHAEL PETRANEK
JIM SALICRUP
Editor-in-Chief

ISBN: 978-1-59707-338-7 paperback edition
ISBN: 978-1-59707-339-4 hardcover edition

Printed in Canada
October 2012 by Friesens Printing
1 Printers Way
Altona, MB R0G 0B0

Distributed by Macmillan

First Printing

MEET SABAN'S POWER RANGERS SUPER SAMURAI

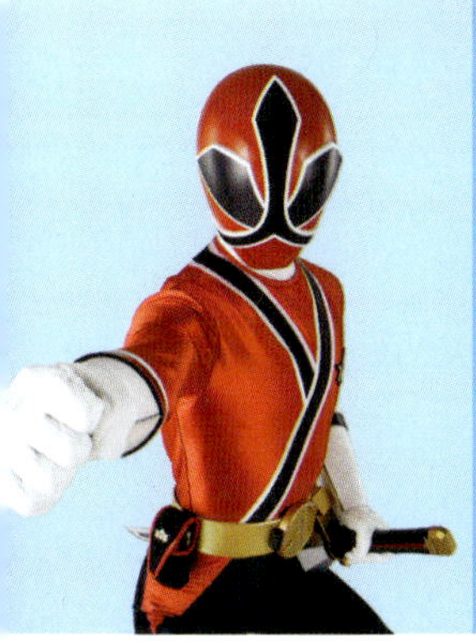

For as long as the Nighlok have existed, there have been Power Rangers sworn to fight them.

The current team of Samurai Power Rangers is a group of teens who grew up knowing that one day they would be summoned to use their uniquely inherited powers and extraordinary skills against evil as the Power Rangers. These skills and powers have been passed down through generation to generation and determine which Ranger they will become.

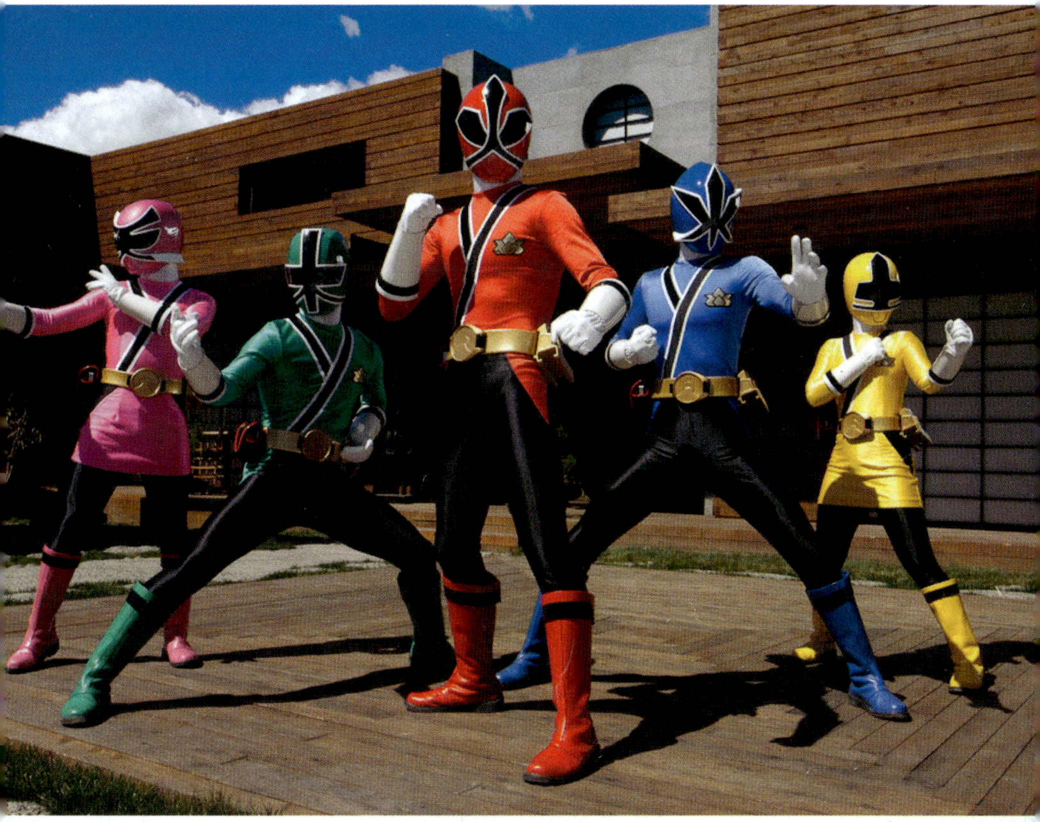

POWER RANGERS SUPER SAMURAI

THE RED RANGER (JAYDEN)

Jayden, the Red Ranger, is the leader of the Samurai Power Rangers. He is a man of few words, but when he speaks he means what he says. He was raised by Mentor Ji after hi father died, who was the Red Ranger befor him. Jayden has become an excellent warri and has kept the Moogers at bay on his own for some time. Now, with the help of the other Rangers, Jayden is learning to be leader and what it is like to have true frienc

Jayden is a kind and caring person but can be firm when action calls. He also carries a secret that he cannot reveal the other Rangers and at times this knowledge causes him conflict.

His element is fire and his Zord is the Lion.

Weapon:
Spin Sword/Fire Smasher

Signature Move:
Fire Smasher!

Element:
Fire

Zord:
Lion

Notes:
Trained to be a Samurai from a very young age.

THE PINK RANGER (MIA)

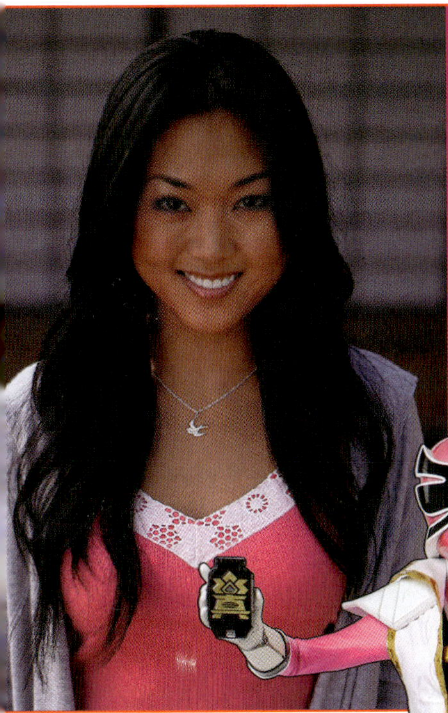

Mia, the Pink Ranger, is the big sister to the group. She is a confident, intuitive, and sensitive person. She is very pragmatic and cares a lot about the well-being of the other Rangers. She trains as hard as the rest of the team, and will jump in to help any Ranger or person in need.

Mia enjoys cooking and often offers up her skills to feed the other Rangers. Problem is that Mia is not a good cook. The humor begins as the other Rangers try their best to act as if her culinary delights are edible.

Mia's element is the sky and her Zord is the Turtle.

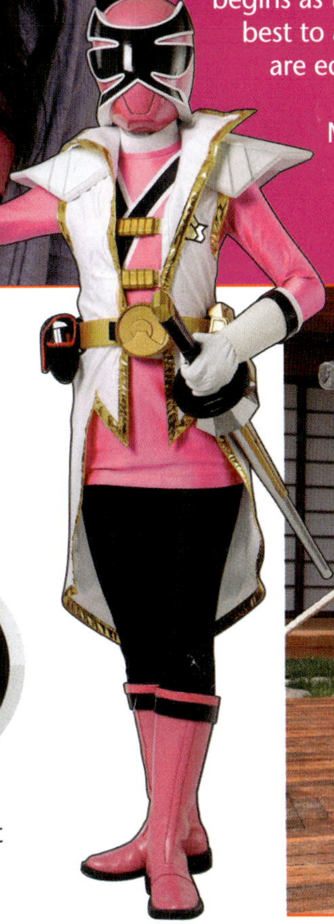

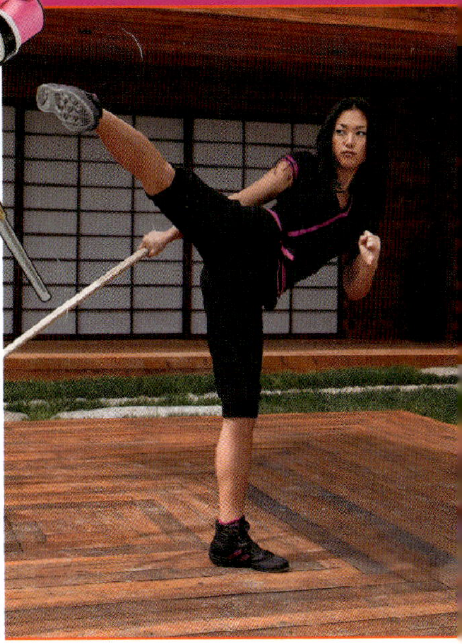

Weapon:
Spin Sword/Sky Fan

Signature Move:
Airway!

Element:
Sky

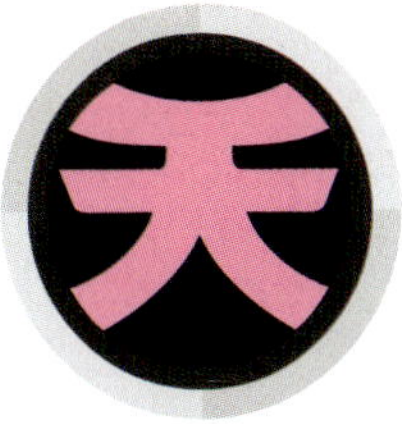
天

Zord:
Turtle

Notes:
Longs to be a gourmet chef and used to sing

SABAN'S POWER RANGERS SUPER SAMURAI

THE BLUE RANGER (KEVIN)

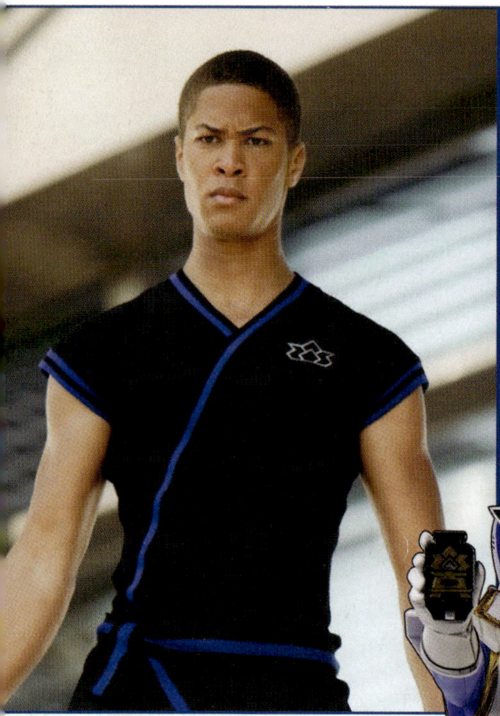

Kevin, the Blue Ranger, has lived his entire life by the code of the Samurai.

Kevin's dream was to be an Olympic swimmer. However, he has placed that dream on hold to become the Blue Ranger. He is a well-trained swordsman and has been raised on the traditions of the Samurai. Kevin is the more sober Ranger who continues his discipline with a daily workout and training. He is honored to be a Samurai and takes his position among the Rangers seriously.

His element is water and his Zord is the Dragon.

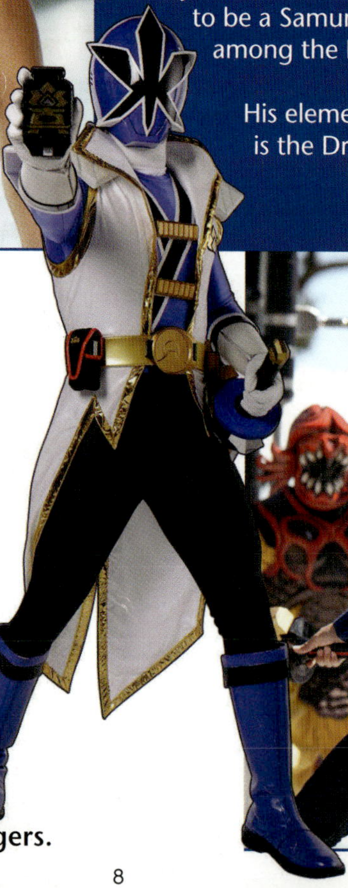

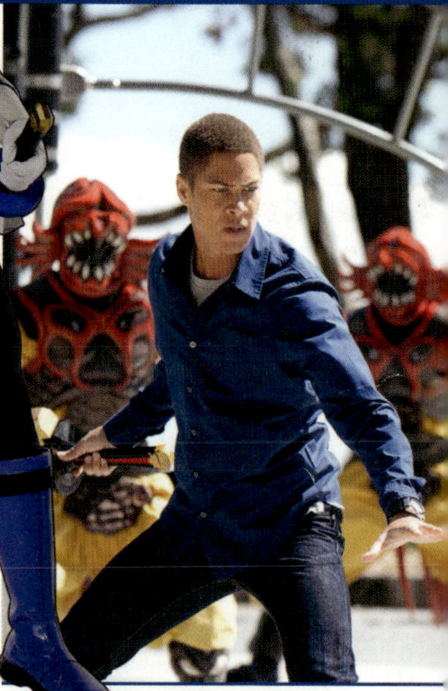

Weapon:
Spin Sword/Hydro Bow

Signature Move:
Dragon Splash!

Element:
Water

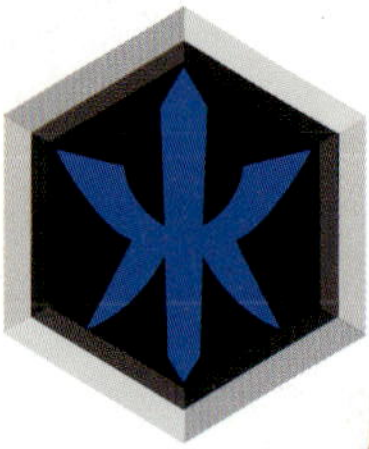

Zord:
Dragon

Notes:
Aside from Jayden, Kevin has the best technique of all the Rangers.

THE GREEN RANGER (MIKE)

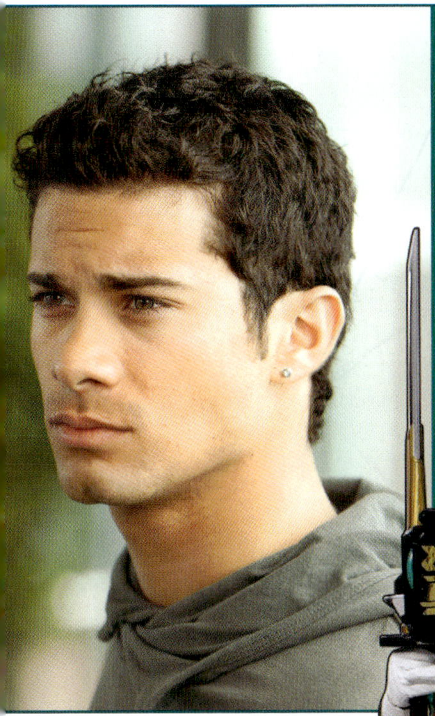

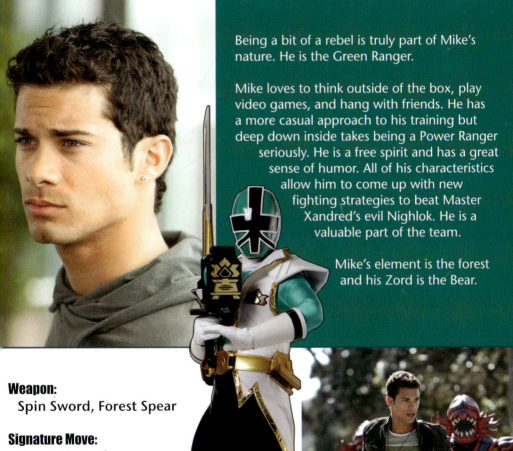

Being a bit of a rebel is truly part of Mike's nature. He is the Green Ranger.

Mike loves to think outside of the box, play video games, and hang with friends. He has a more casual approach to his training but deep down inside takes being a Power Ranger seriously. He is a free spirit and has a great sense of humor. All of his characteristics allow him to come up with new fighting strategies to beat Master Xandred's evil Nighlok. He is a valuable part of the team.

Mike's element is the forest and his Zord is the Bear.

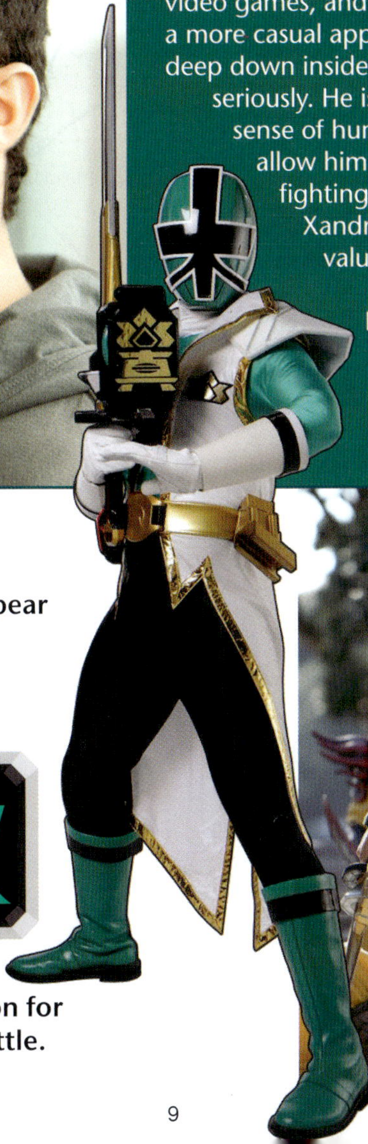

Weapon:
Spin Sword, Forest Spear

Signature Move:
Forest Vortex!

Element:
Forest

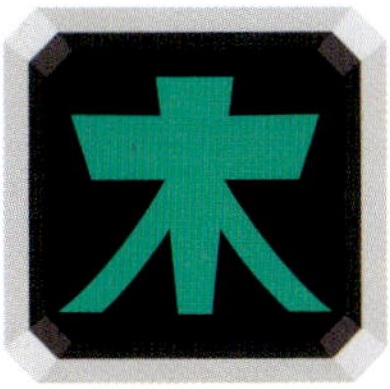
木

Zord:
Bear

Notes:
Mike has a reputation for being creative in battle.

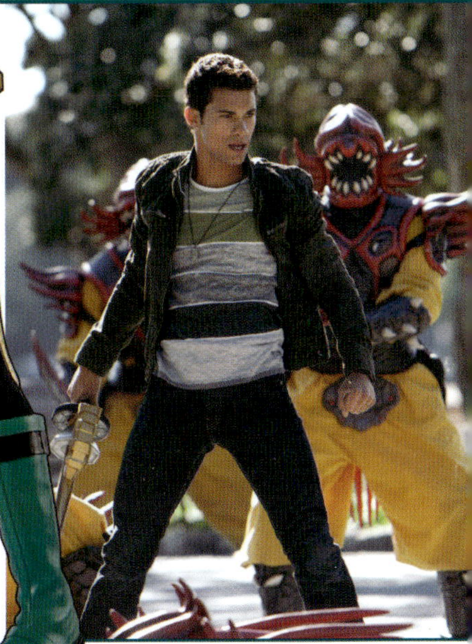

THE YELLOW RANGER (EMILY)

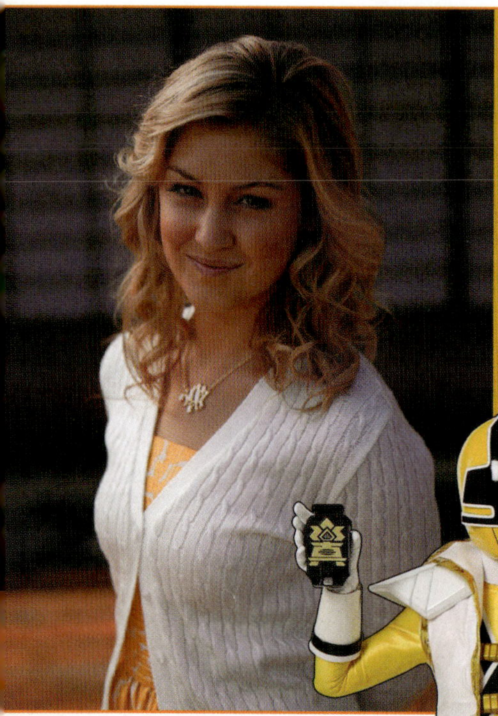

Youngest of the Rangers, Emily is the Yellow Ranger. She is a sweet and kind person who was raised in the countryside.

It was actually her sister who was originally to become the Yellow Ranger prior to falling ill. Emily stepped up to the challenge and took her sister's spot on the team. She is determined to make her sister proud and trains harder because of that. She is very musical, and her silliness is infectious. Her wide-eyed optimism often helps the team stay positive when it seems that all the odds are against them.

Emily's element is Earth and her Zord is the Ape.

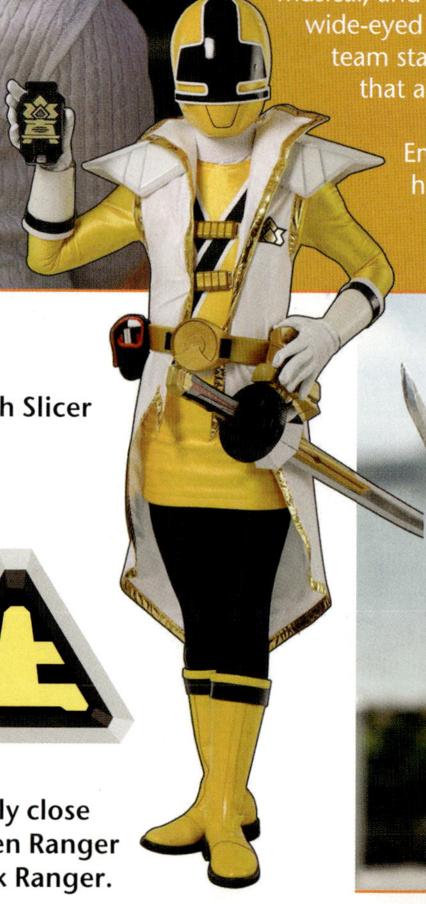

Weapon:
Spin Sword/Earth Slicer

Signature Move:
Seismic Swing!

Element:
Earth

Zord:
Ape

Notes:
Emily is especially close to Mike the Green Ranger and Mia the Pink Ranger.

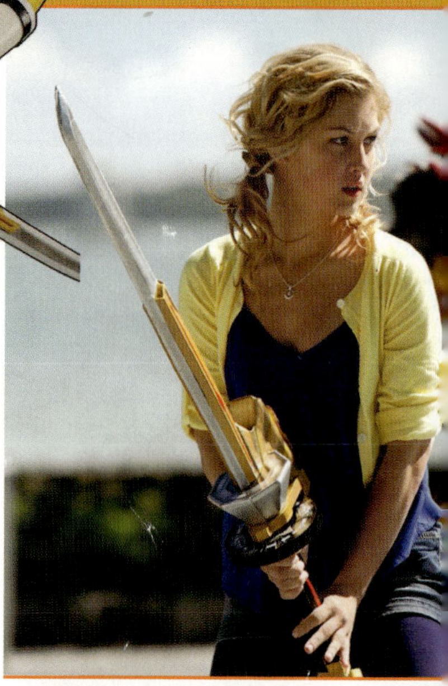

SABAN'S POWER RANGERS SUPER SAMURAI

THE GOLD RANGER (ANTONIO)

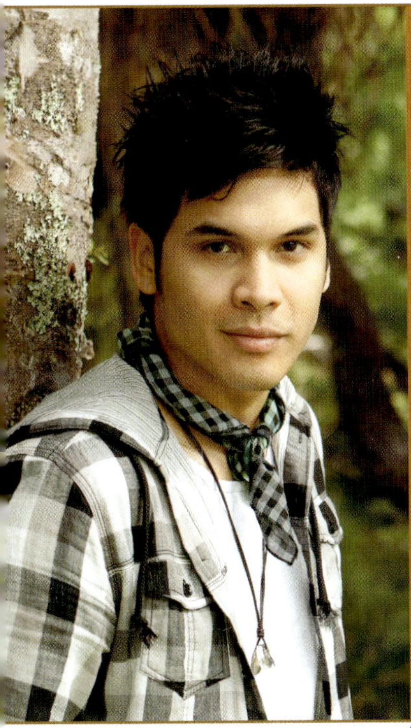

Antonio is not like the rest of the Power Rangers and is uniquely the Gold Ranger.

Unlike the other five Power Rangers, Antonio did not receive any formal Samurai training and mastered his fighting skills on his own. When he was a young child, he and Jayden were best friends. They practiced the Samurai moves together, but then Antonio's family moved away. Antonio vowed to return and to become a Samurai Power Ranger. Using his computer skills, Antonio was able to create his own Samuraizer, able to program powers and operate his OctoZord which was a present from Jayden years before. True to his word, Antonio returns as the Gold Ranger with mastered samurai skills.

His element is light and his Zord is an Octopus known as OctoZord.

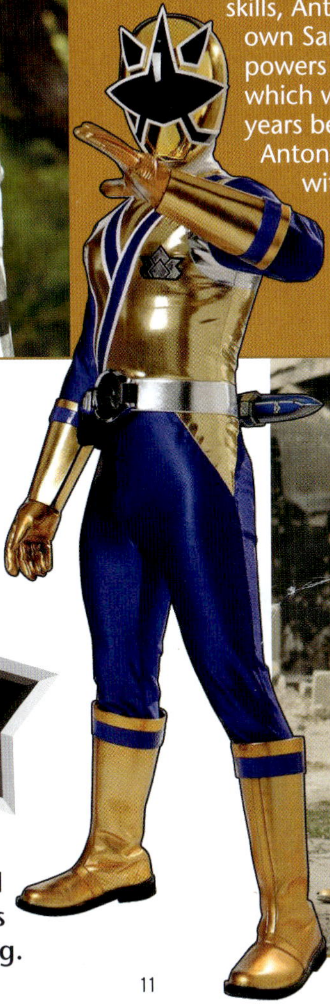

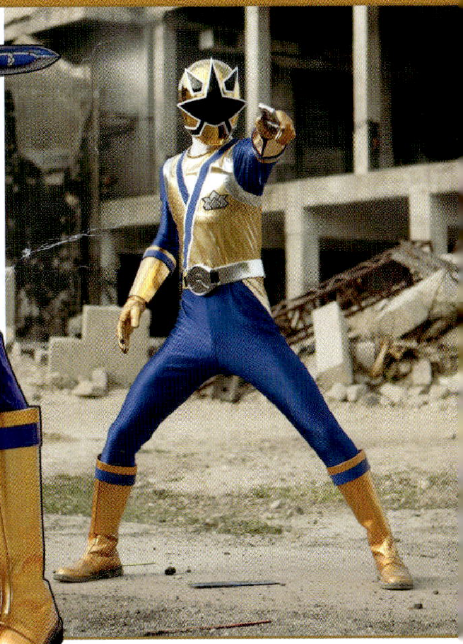

Weapon:
Barracuda Blade

Signature Move:
Barracuda Bite!

Element:
Light

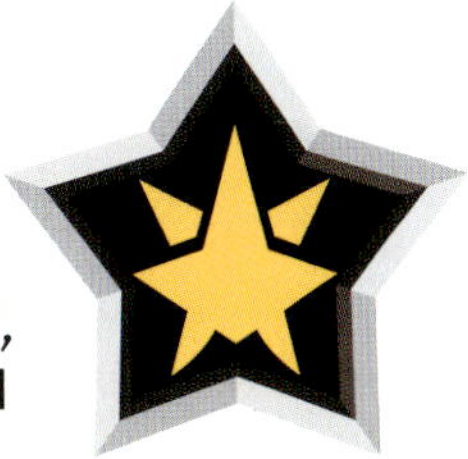

Zord:
OctoZord,
LightZord

Notes:
Antonio is a techie and communicates with his Zord via text messaging.

MASTER XANDRED

Master Xandred is the leader of the Nighlok Monsters who inhabit the Netherworld.

Jayden's Father, the previous Red Ranger, shattered Master Xandred into a million pieces, vanishing him to the Netherworld forever. Recently Master Xandred awoke and began a reign of terror in an attempt to return to our world. With his trusty advisor, Master Xandred has sent Nighlok to Earth in an attempt to make the humans cry as their tears hel raise the Sanzu River. Once the river is high enough, Master Xandred can escape the Netherworld and rule the Earth.

OCTOROO

Octoroo is Master Xandred's trusted advisor. He counsels Master Xandred about the Netherworld and the Nighlok that live there. Often he offers up new plans and tactics to defeat the Rangers. Octoroo is an Octopus-like creature and at times cannot be trusted.

DAYU

Dayu has not always been half human and half Nighlok. She once was a new bride. She traded her human life centuries ago in an effort to save her husband as a powerful Nighlok promised to spare her husband if she would go with him. The only possession she was allowed to take with her was her guitar which became the "Harmonium." Master Xandred keeps her near because her music soothes him.

ARE YOU SURE ABOUT THIS, BILL?

DON'T WORRY, HE'LL *LOVE* IT!

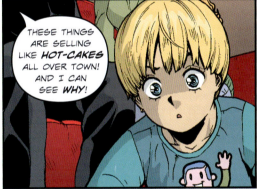

THESE THINGS ARE SELLING LIKE *HOT-CAKES* ALL OVER TOWN! AND I CAN SEE *WHY*!

HEY, IT EVEN MOVES! LOOK AT THAT SUCKER *GO*!

SEE? HE LIKES IT!

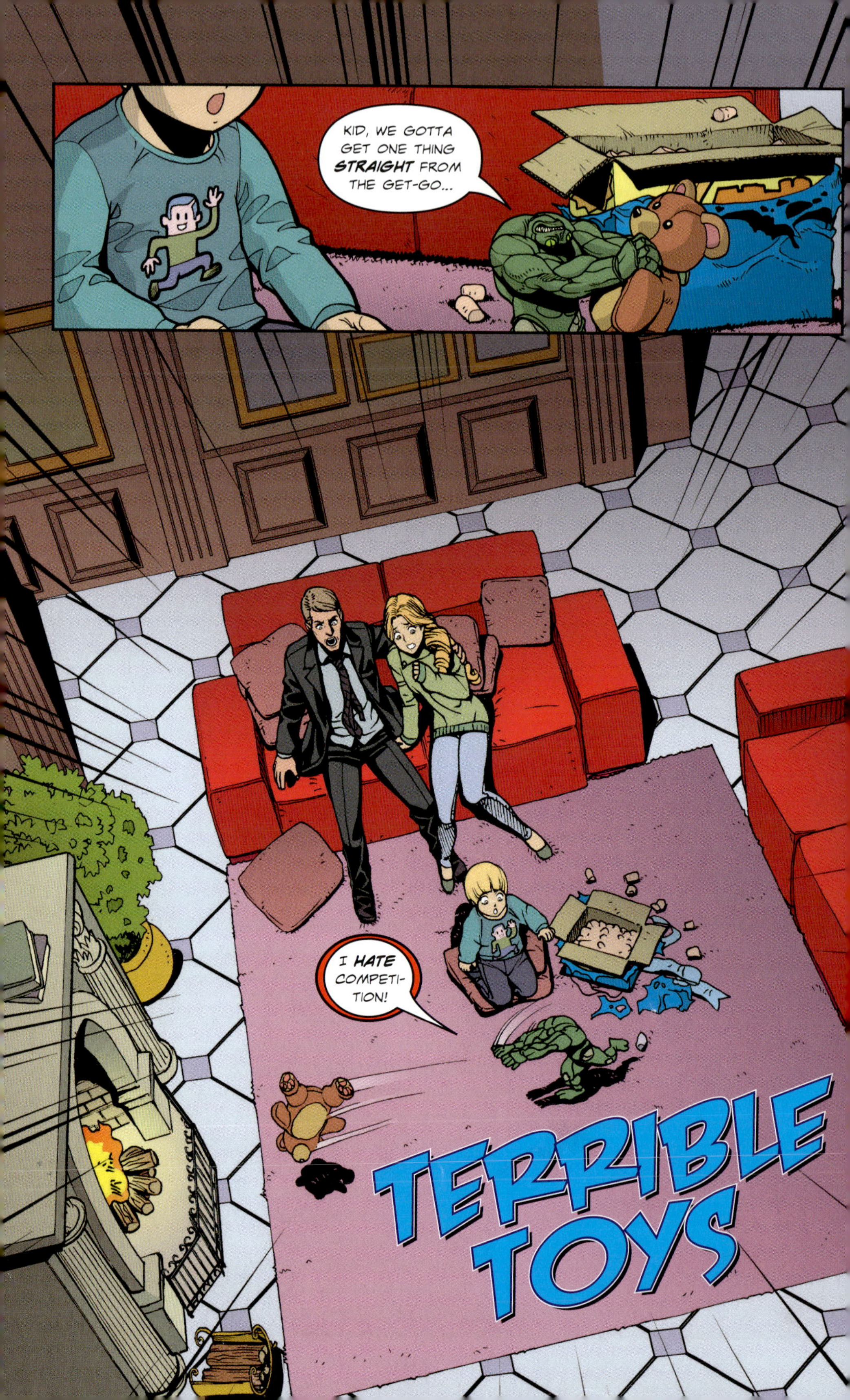
KID, WE GOTTA GET ONE THING STRAIGHT FROM THE GET-GO...
I HATE COMPETI-TION!
TERRIBLE TOYS

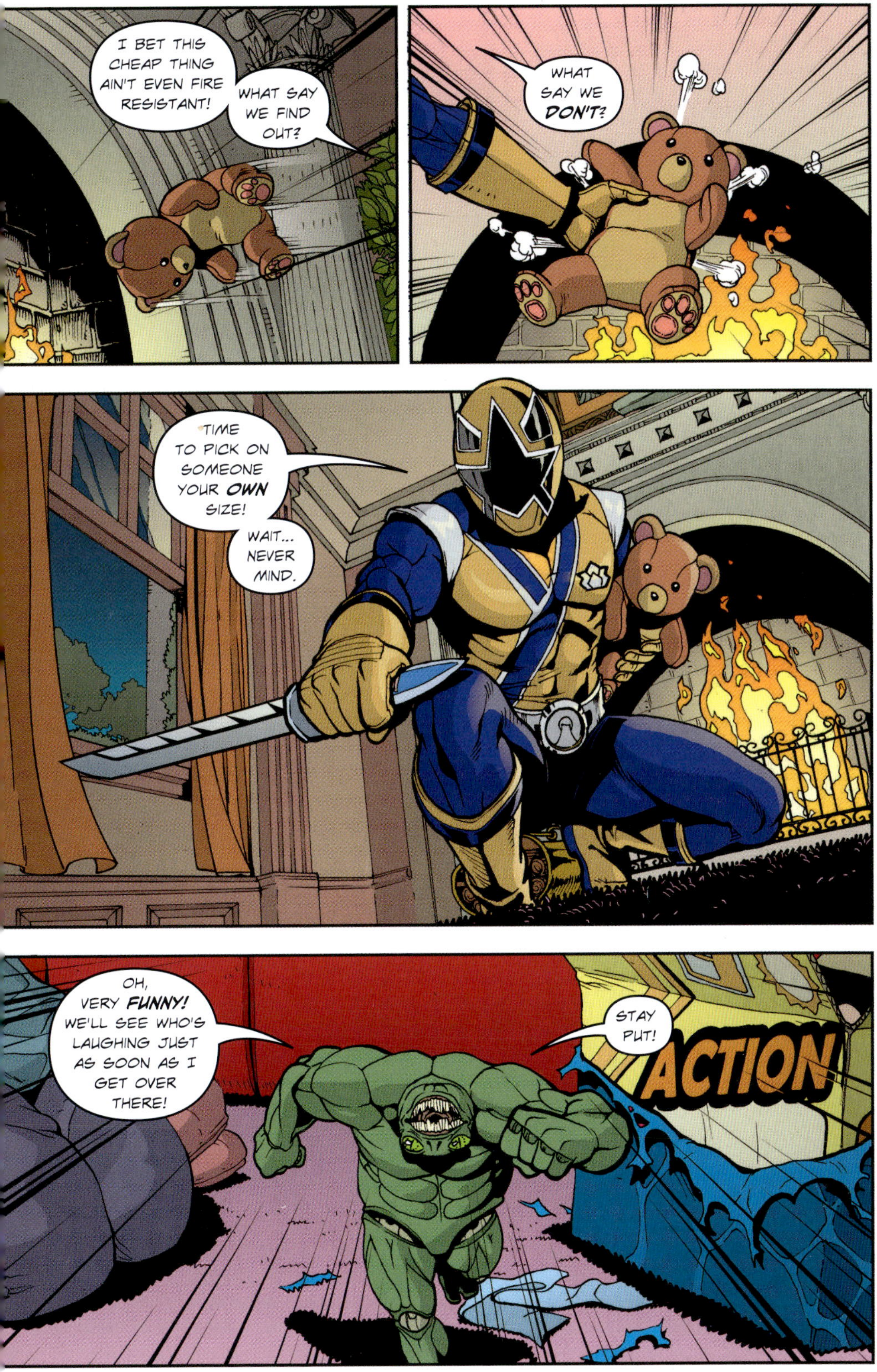
I BET THIS CHEAP THING AIN'T EVEN FIRE RESISTANT!
WHAT SAY WE FIND OUT?
WHAT SAY WE DON'T?
TIME TO PICK ON SOMEONE YOUR OWN SIZE!
WAIT... NEVER MIND.
OH, VERY FUNNY! WE'LL SEE WHO'S LAUGHING JUST AS SOON AS I GET OVER THERE!
STAY PUT!
ACTION

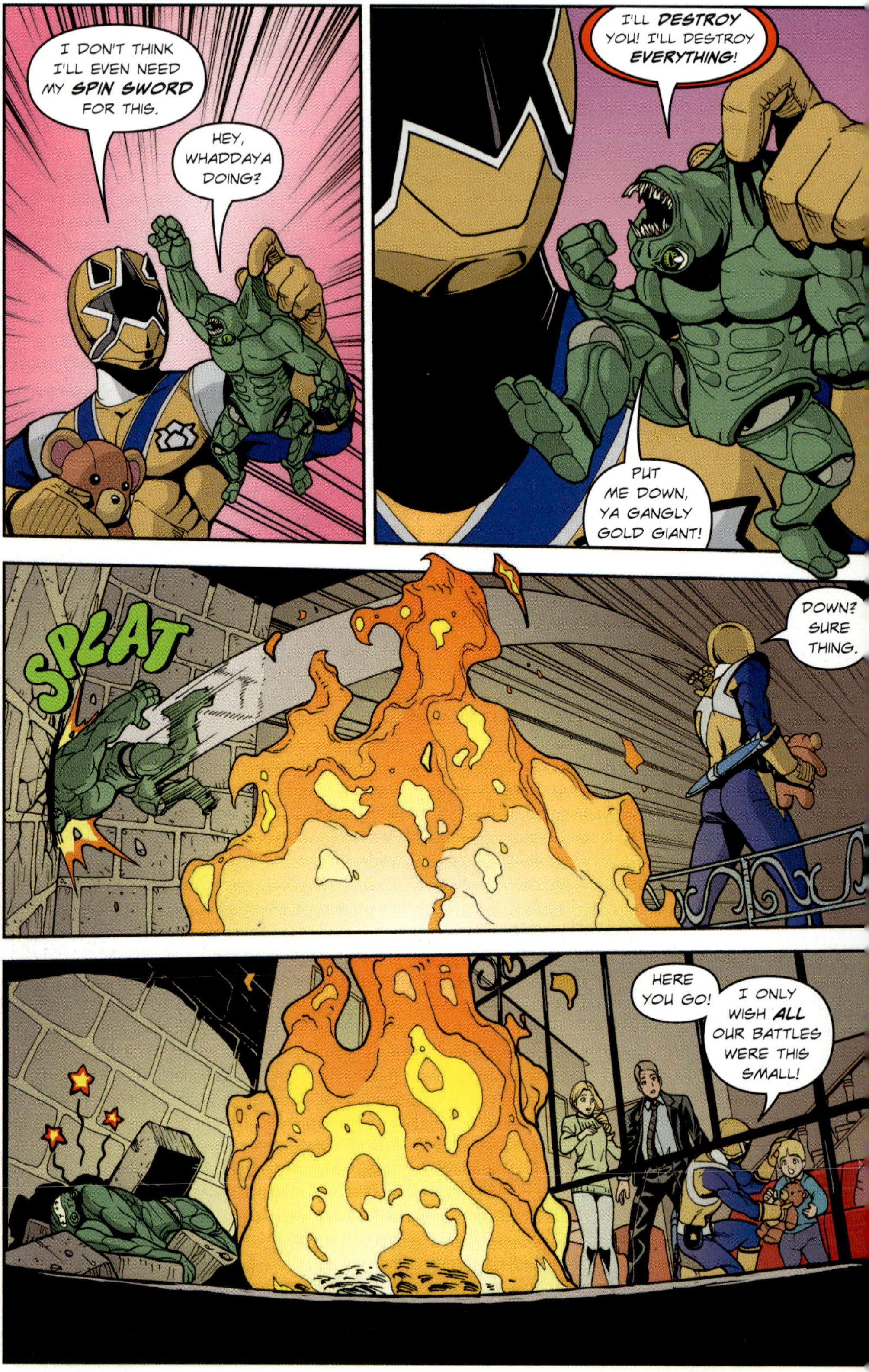

I DON'T THINK I'LL EVEN NEED MY SPIN SWORD FOR THIS.
HEY, WHADDAYA DOING?
I'LL DESTROY YOU! I'LL DESTROY EVERYTHING!
PUT ME DOWN, YA GANGLY GOLD GIANT!
SPLAT
DOWN? SURE THING.
HERE YOU GO!
I ONLY WISH ALL OUR BATTLES WERE THIS SMALL!

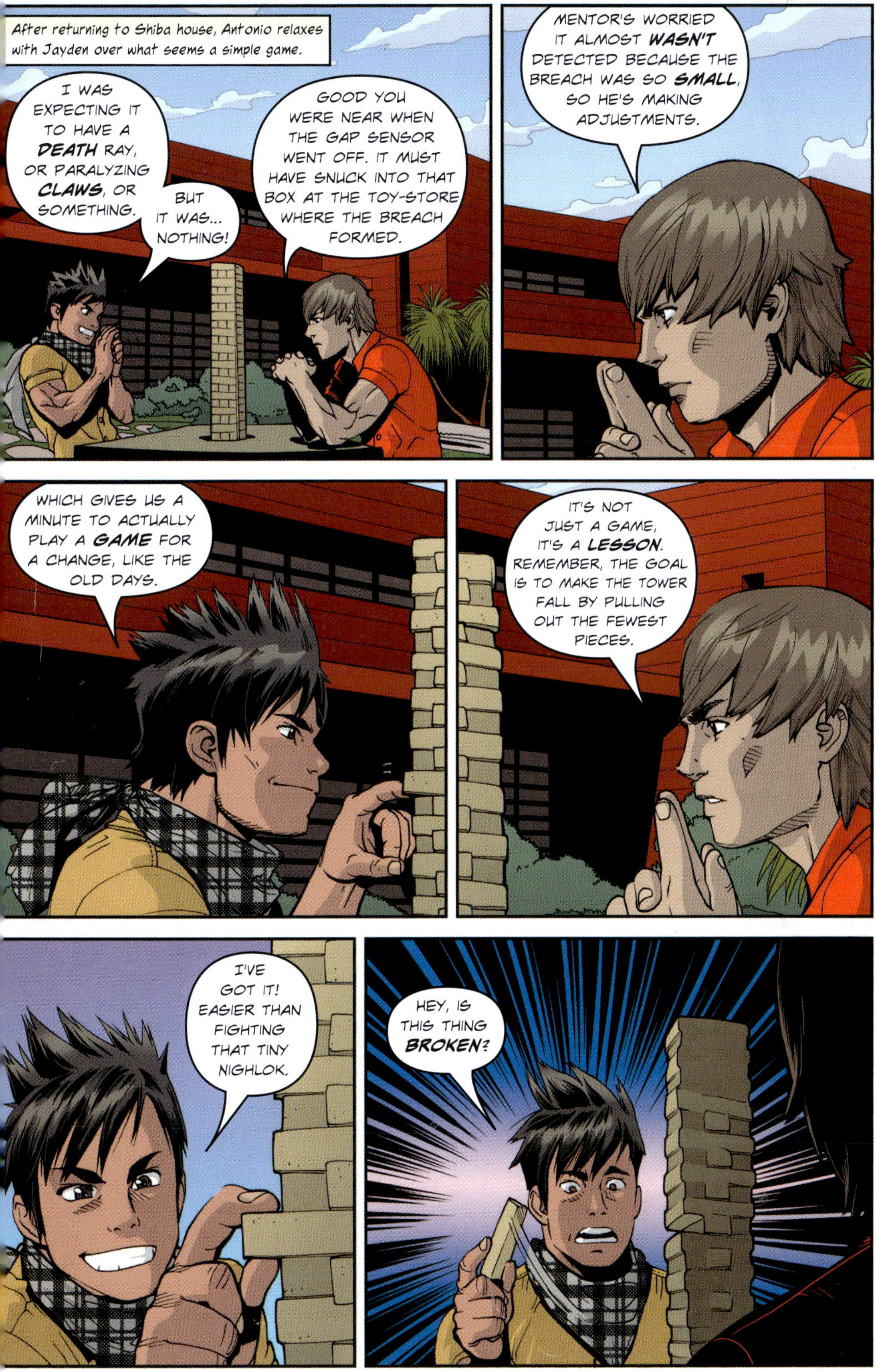
After returning to Shiba house, Antonio relaxes with Jayden over what seems a simple game.
I WAS EXPECTING IT TO HAVE A DEATH RAY, OR PARALYZING CLAWS, OR SOMETHING.
BUT IT WAS... NOTHING!
GOOD YOU WERE NEAR WHEN THE GAP SENSOR WENT OFF. IT MUST HAVE SNUCK INTO THAT BOX AT THE TOY-STORE WHERE THE BREACH FORMED.
MENTOR'S WORRIED IT ALMOST WASN'T DETECTED BECAUSE THE BREACH WAS SO SMALL, SO HE'S MAKING ADJUSTMENTS.
WHICH GIVES US A MINUTE TO ACTUALLY PLAY A GAME FOR A CHANGE, LIKE THE OLD DAYS.
IT'S NOT JUST A GAME, IT'S A LESSON. REMEMBER, THE GOAL IS TO MAKE THE TOWER FALL BY PULLING OUT THE FEWEST PIECES.
I'VE GOT IT! EASIER THAN FIGHTING THAT TINY NIGHLOK.
HEY, IS THIS THING BROKEN?

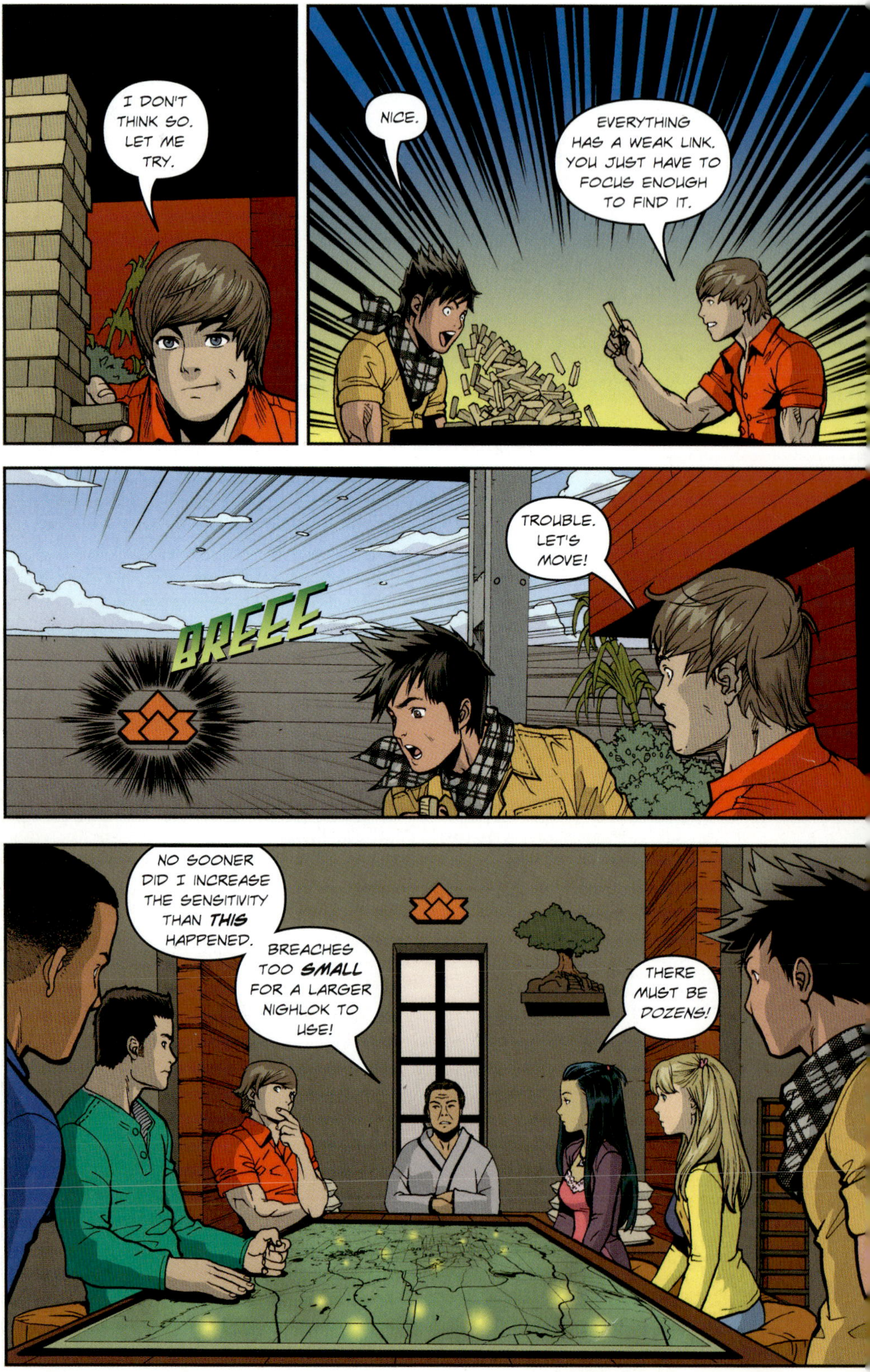
I DON'T THINK SO. LET ME TRY.
NICE.
EVERYTHING HAS A WEAK LINK. YOU JUST HAVE TO FOCUS ENOUGH TO FIND IT.
BREEE
TROUBLE. LET'S MOVE!
NO SOONER DID I INCREASE THE SENSITIVITY THAN *THIS* HAPPENED.
BREACHES TOO **SMALL** FOR A LARGER NIGHLOK TO USE!
THERE MUST BE DOZENS!

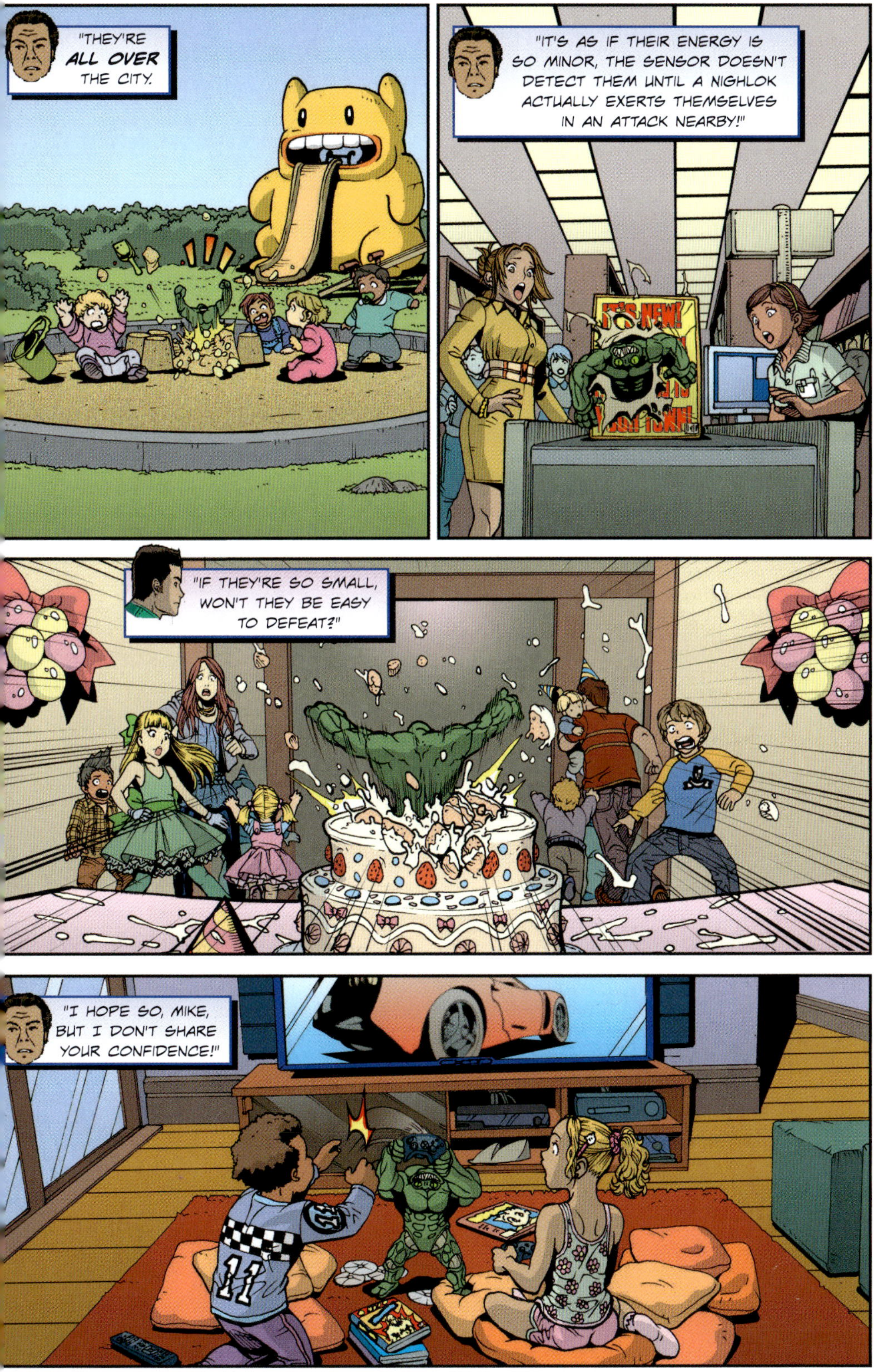
"THEY'RE ALL OVER THE CITY.
"IT'S AS IF THEIR ENERGY IS SO MINOR, THE SENSOR DOESN'T DETECT THEM UNTIL A NIGHLOK ACTUALLY EXERTS THEMSELVES IN AN ATTACK NEARBY!"
"IF THEY'RE SO SMALL, WON'T THEY BE EASY TO DEFEAT?"
"I HOPE SO, MIKE, BUT I DON'T SHARE YOUR CONFIDENCE!"

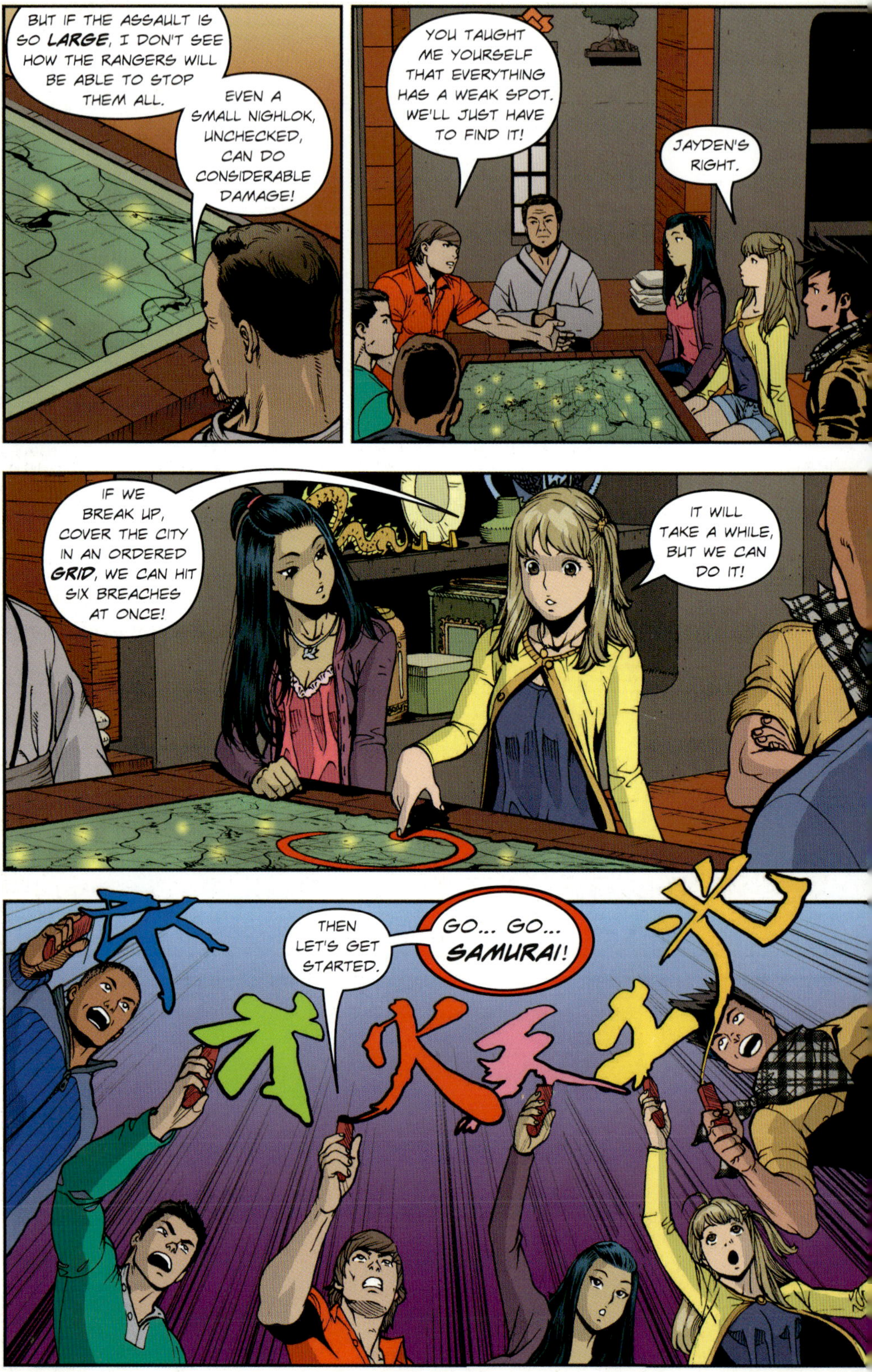
BUT IF THE ASSAULT IS SO LARGE, I DON'T SEE HOW THE RANGERS WILL BE ABLE TO STOP THEM ALL.
EVEN A SMALL NIGHLOK, UNCHECKED, CAN DO CONSIDERABLE DAMAGE!
YOU TAUGHT ME YOURSELF THAT EVERYTHING HAS A WEAK SPOT. WE'LL JUST HAVE TO FIND IT!
JAYDEN'S RIGHT.
IF WE BREAK UP, COVER THE CITY IN AN ORDERED GRID, WE CAN HIT SIX BREACHES AT ONCE!
IT WILL TAKE A WHILE, BUT WE CAN DO IT!
THEN LET'S GET STARTED.
GO... GO... SAMURAI!

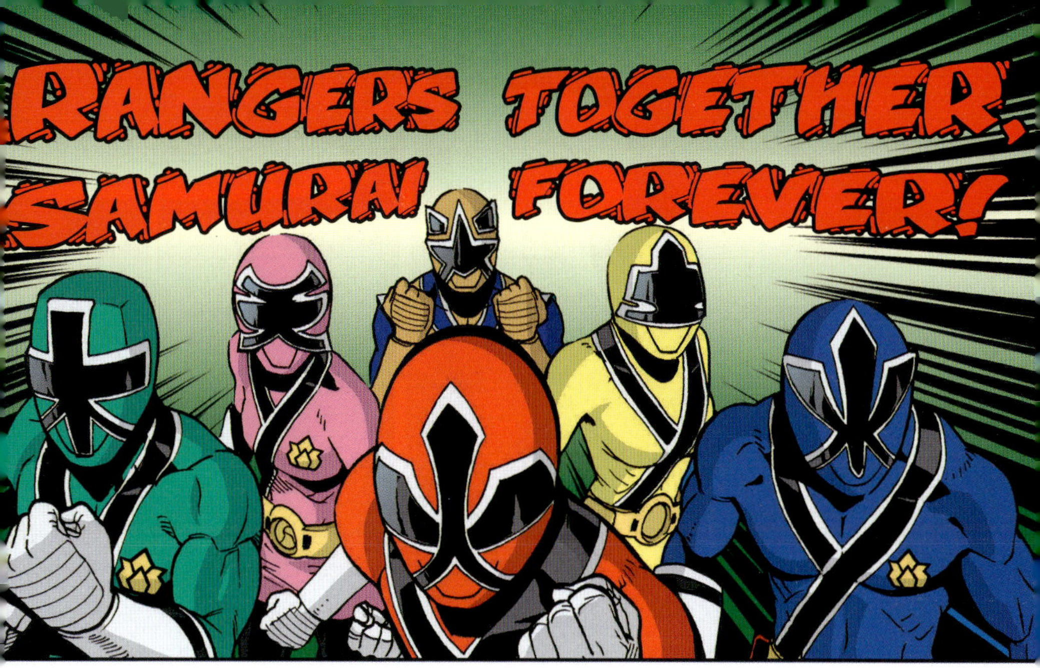
RANGERS TOGETHER, SAMURAI FOREVER!

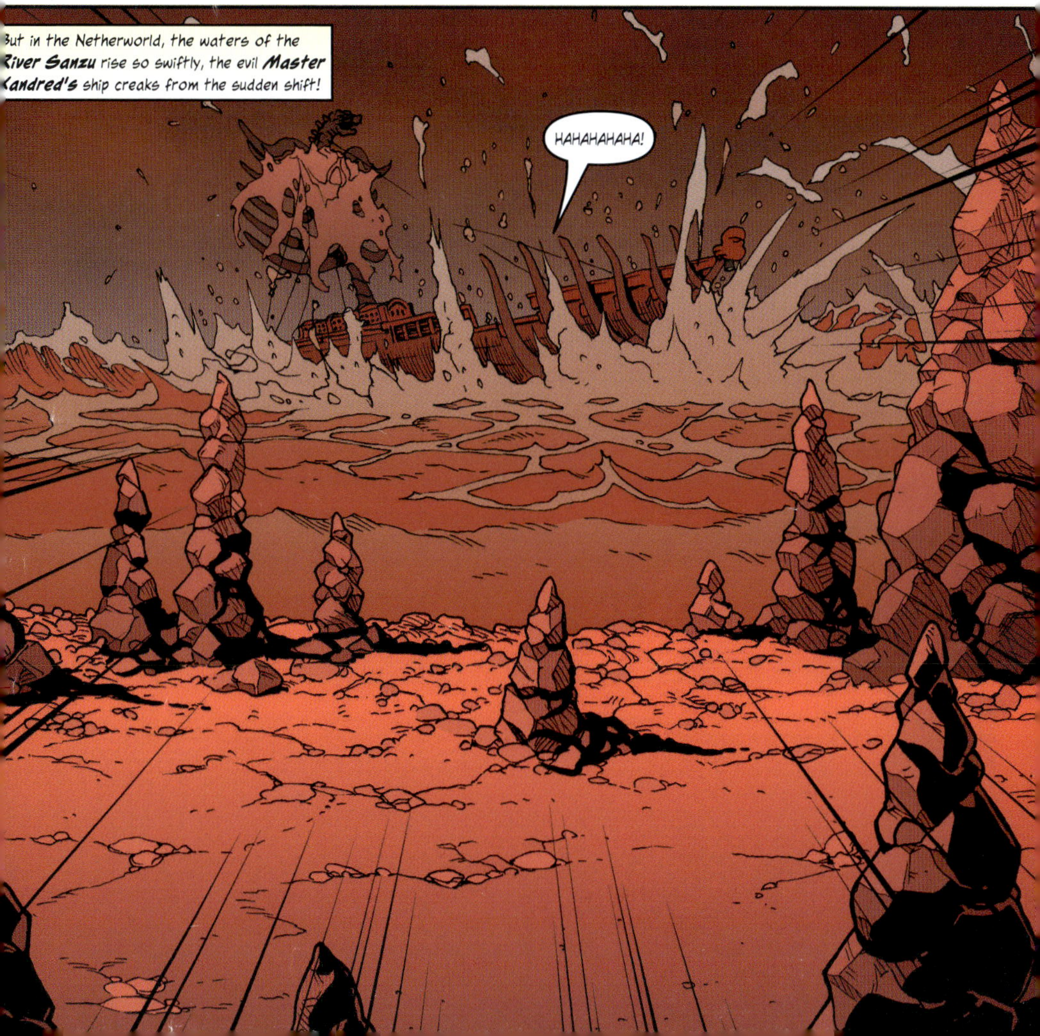
But in the Netherworld, the waters of the River Sanzu rise so swiftly, the evil Master Xandred's ship creaks from the sudden shift!
HAHAHAHAHA!

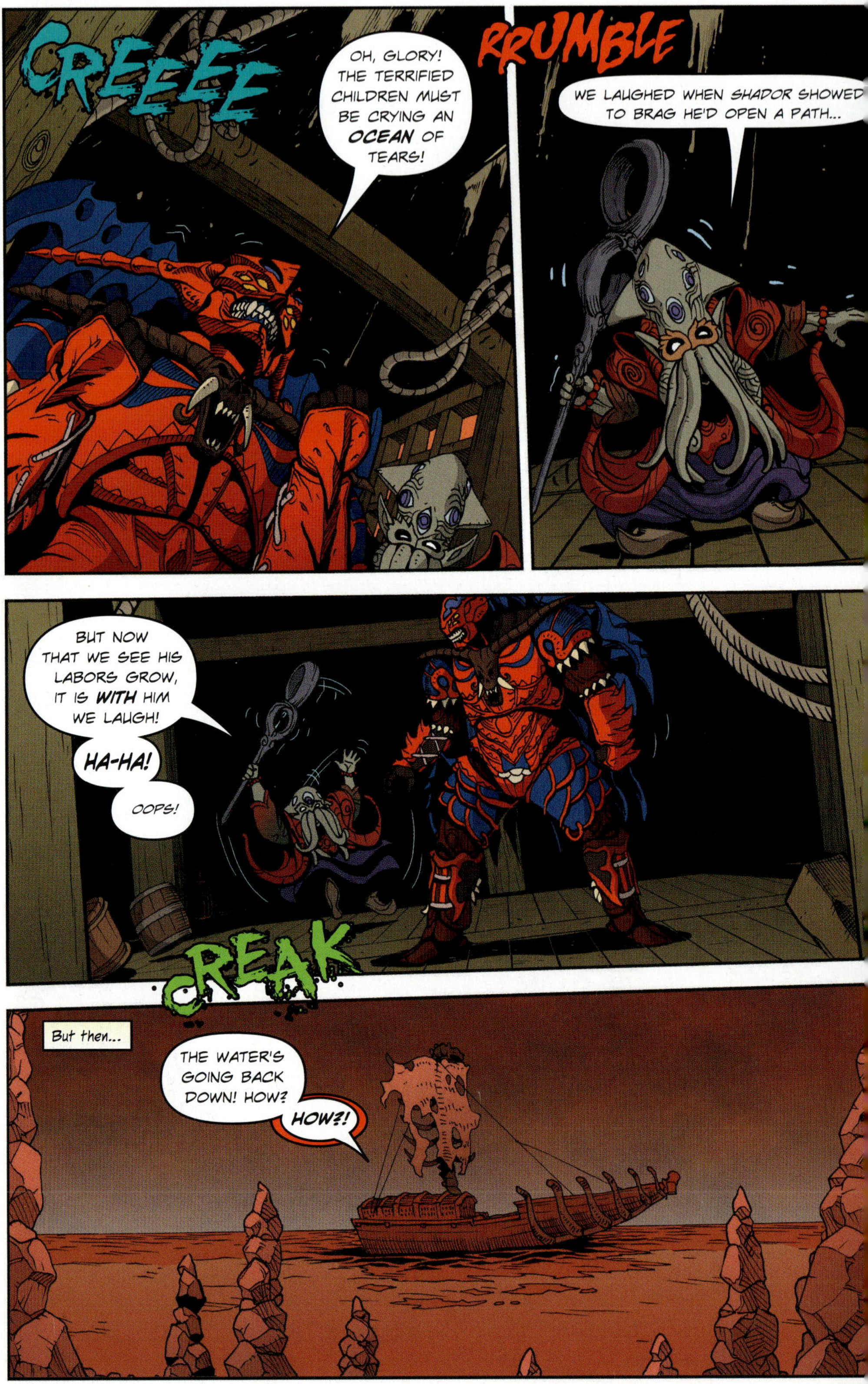
CREEEE
OH, GLORY! THE TERRIFIED CHILDREN MUST BE CRYING AN OCEAN OF TEARS!
RRUMBLE
WE LAUGHED WHEN SHADOR SHOWED TO BRAG HE'D OPEN A PATH...
BUT NOW THAT WE SEE HIS LABORS GROW, IT IS WITH HIM WE LAUGH!
HA-HA!
OOPS!
CREAK
But then...
THE WATER'S GOING BACK DOWN! HOW?
HOW?!

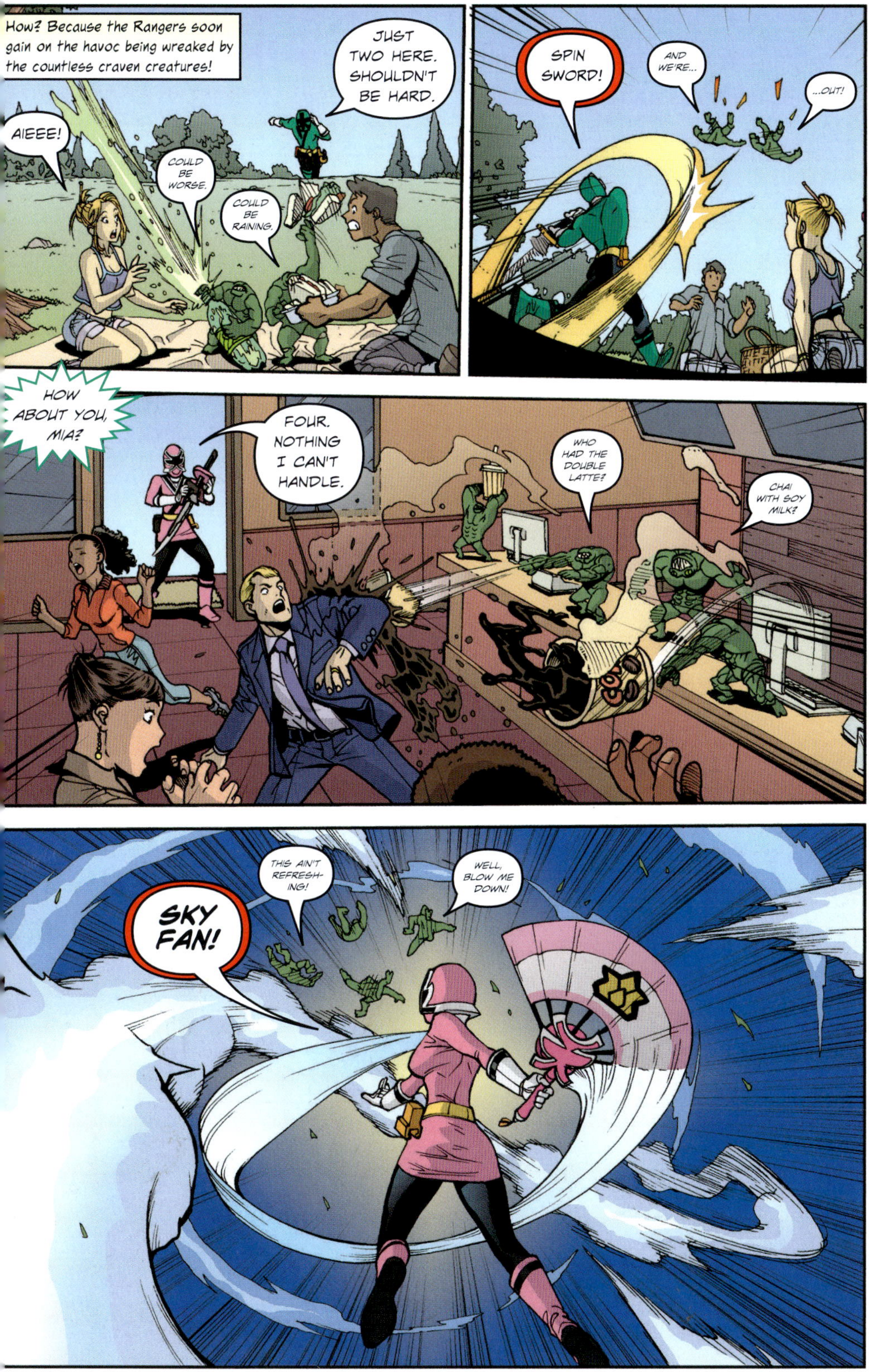
How? Because the Rangers soon gain on the havoc being wreaked by the countless craven creatures!
JUST TWO HERE. SHOULDN'T BE HARD.
AIEEE!
COULD BE WORSE.
COULD BE RAINING.
SPIN SWORD!
AND WE'RE...
...OUT!
HOW ABOUT YOU, MIA?
FOUR. NOTHING I CAN'T HANDLE.
WHO HAD THE DOUBLE LATTE?
CHAI WITH SOY MILK?
SKY FAN!
THIS AIN'T REFRESH-ING!
WELL, BLOW ME DOWN!

IT'S A LITTLE TOUGHER HERE. I'VE GOT *EIGHT*.

BUT I ALSO HAVE *OCTOZORD!*

HAVE A BALL!

HAVE 'EM ALL!

KANJI SYMBOL *ENLARGE!*

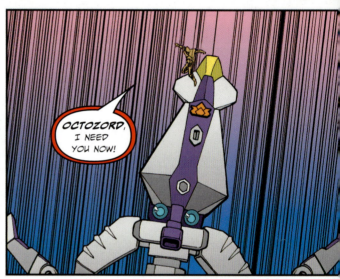

OCTOZORD, I NEED YOU NOW!

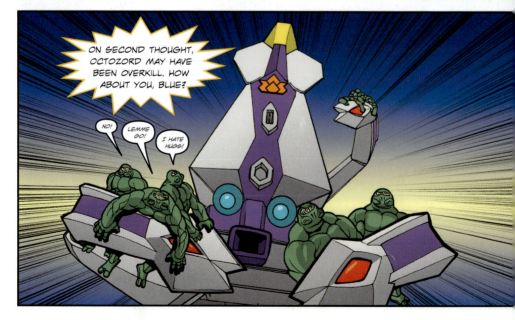

ON SECOND THOUGHT, OCTOZORD MAY HAVE BEEN OVERKILL. HOW ABOUT YOU, BLUE?

NO!

LEMME GO!

I HATE HUGS!

I'VE GOT SIXTEEN AT THE WATER PARK, BUT I THINK I CAN HANDLE IT!
HYDRO-BOW!
COWA-BUNGA!
WAVE BYE-BYE!
HANG TEN!
AND YOU, EMILY?
THIRTY-TWO! I DON'T LIKE THE WAY THIS IS ADDING UP!
LOUSY DRIVERS!
I'M WALKIN' HERE!
ONE SIDE! ONE SIDE!
GLAD I BORROWED THE BULL-ZOOKA.
REMEMBER WHEN JAYDEN USED THAT AGAINST THE MASTER BLASTERS?
OF COURSE! THAT'S WHY I BORROWED IT!

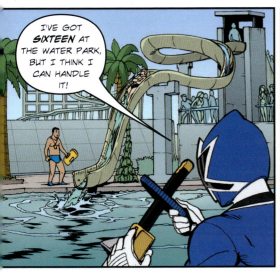

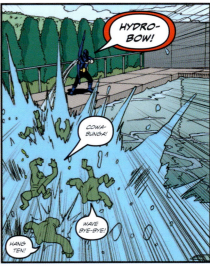

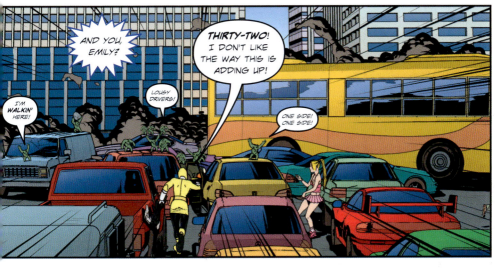

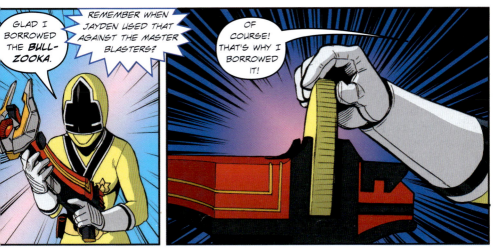

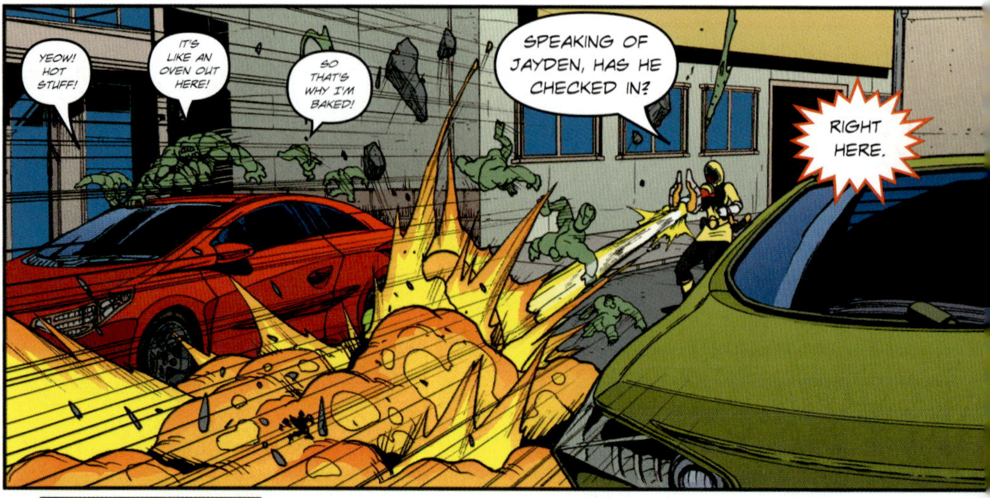
YEOW! HOT STUFF!
IT'S LIKE AN OVEN OUT HERE!
SO THAT'S WHY I'M BAKED!
SPEAKING OF JAYDEN, HAS HE CHECKED IN?
RIGHT HERE.

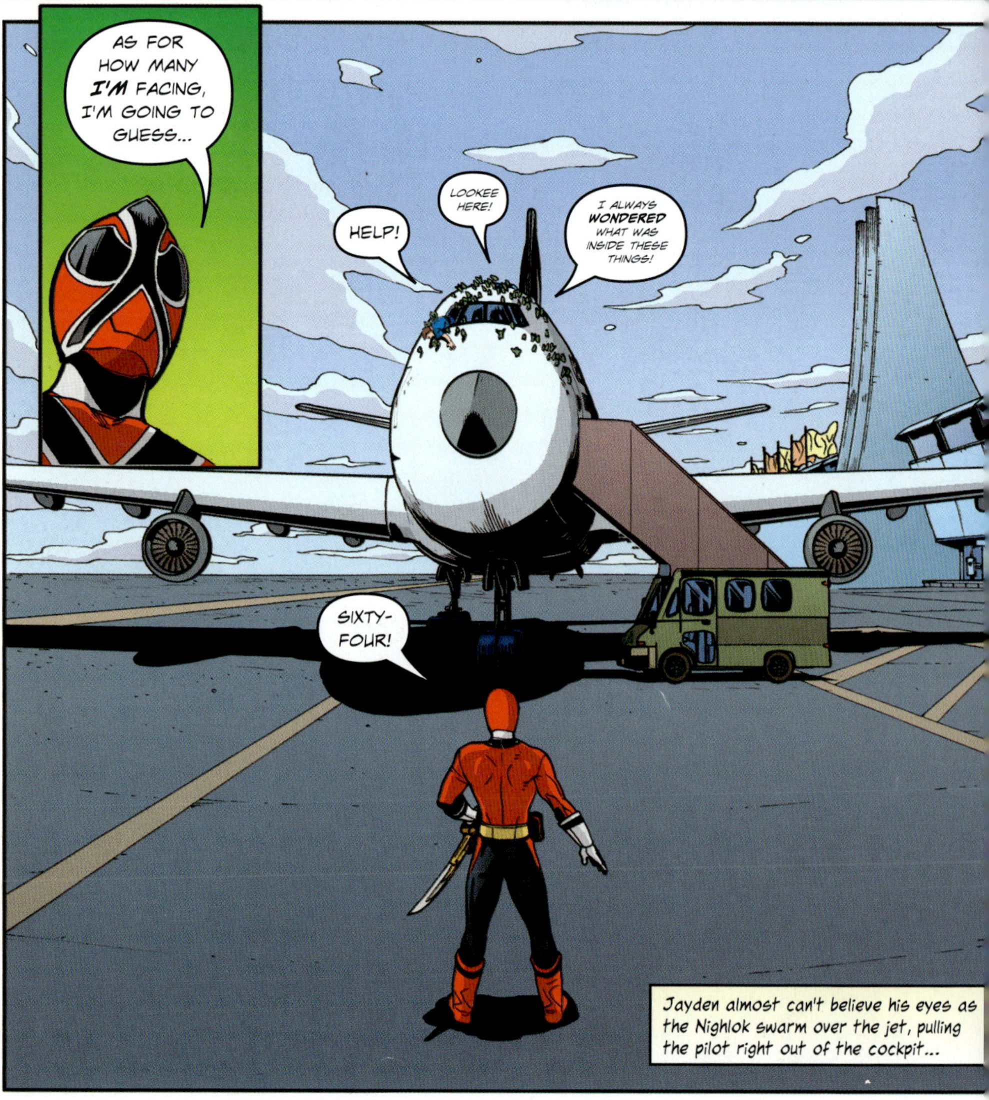
AS FOR HOW MANY I'M FACING, I'M GOING TO GUESS...
HELP!
LOOKEE HERE!
I ALWAYS WONDERED WHAT WAS INSIDE THESE THINGS!
SIXTY-FOUR!
Jayden almost can't believe his eyes as the Nighlok swarm over the jet, pulling the pilot right out of the cockpit...

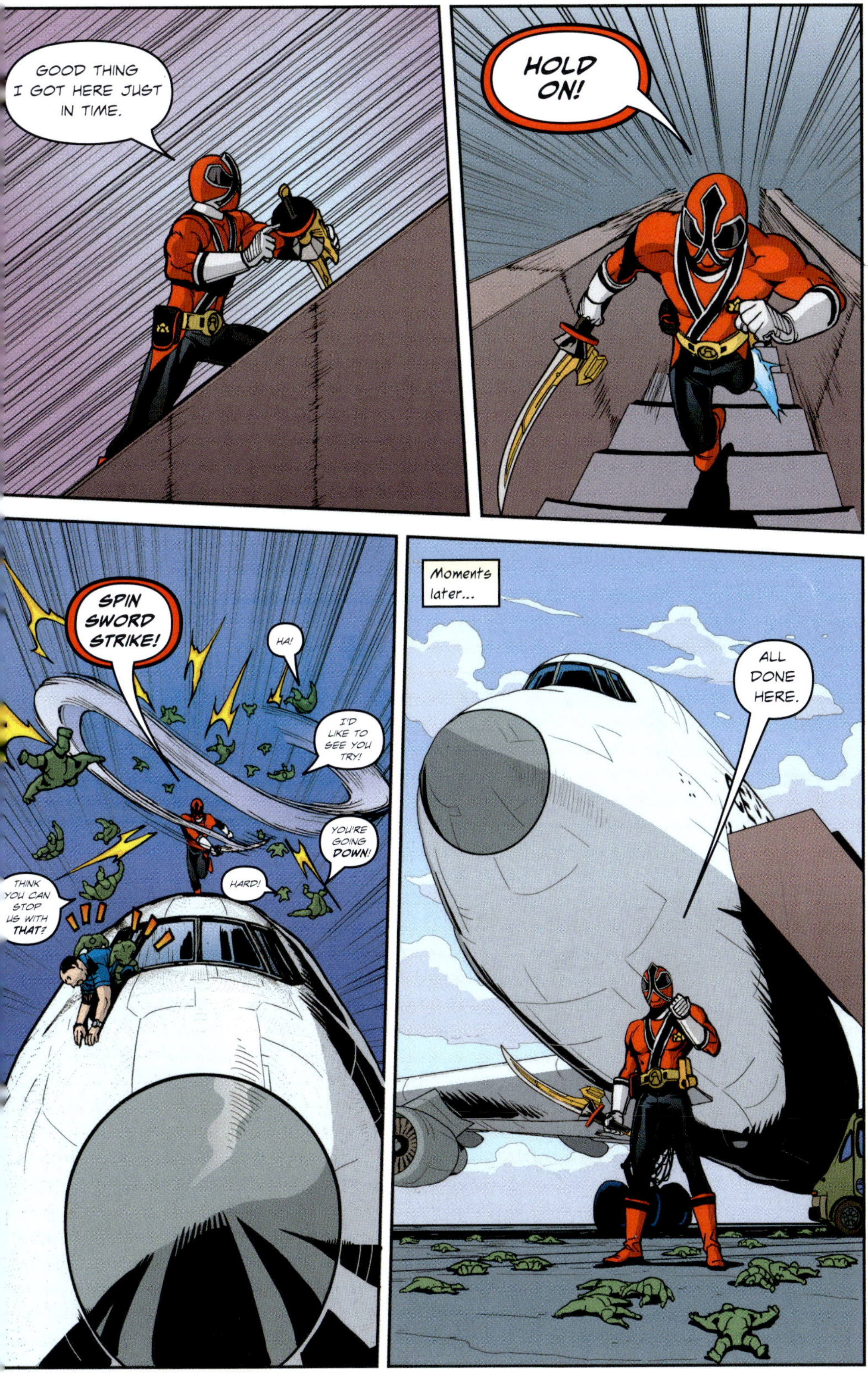
GOOD THING I GOT HERE JUST IN TIME.
HOLD ON!
SPIN SWORD STRIKE!
HA!
I'D LIKE TO SEE YOU TRY!
YOU'RE GOING DOWN!
HARD!
THINK YOU CAN STOP US WITH THAT?
Moments later...
ALL DONE HERE.

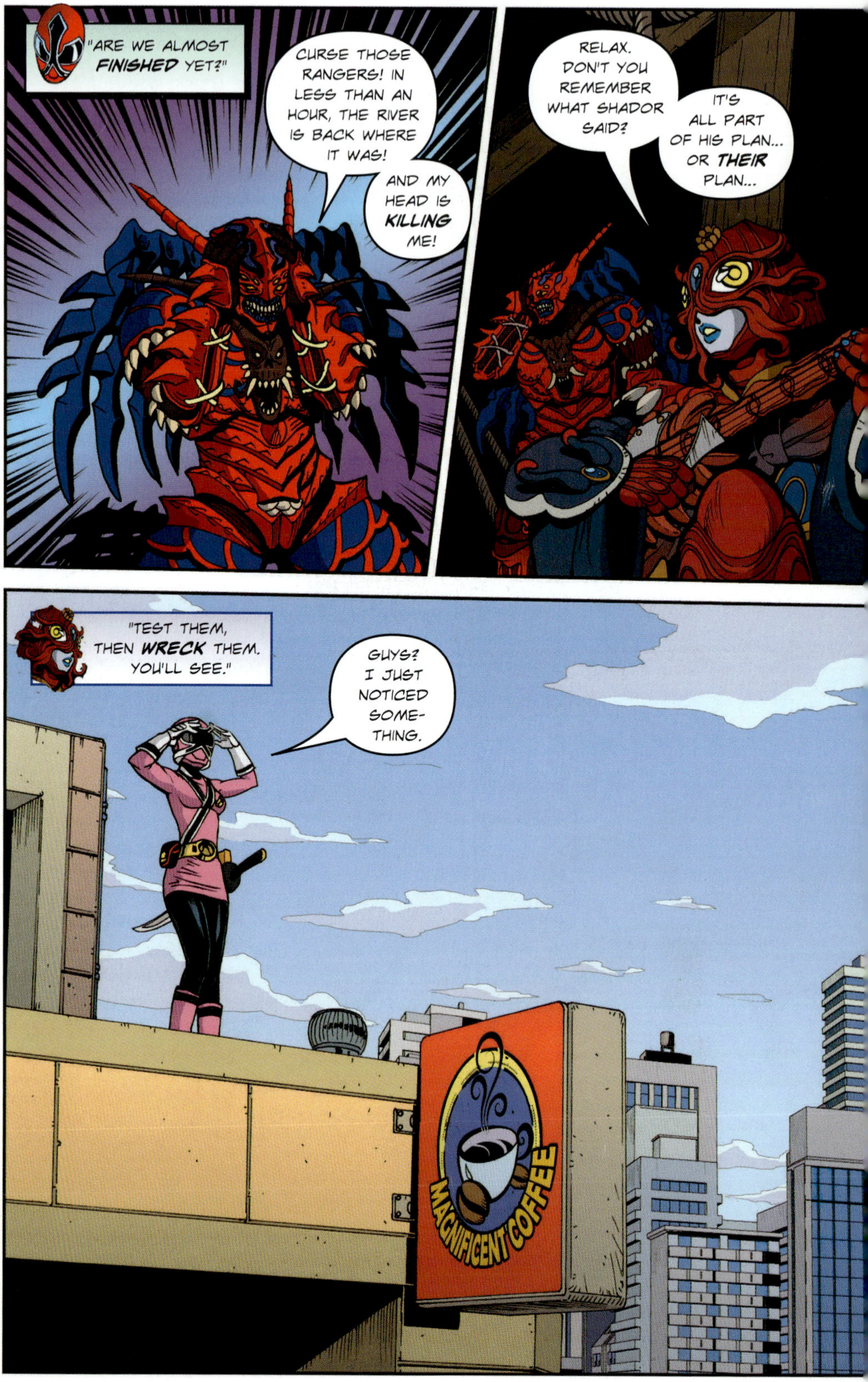
"ARE WE ALMOST FINISHED YET?"
CURSE THOSE RANGERS! IN LESS THAN AN HOUR, THE RIVER IS BACK WHERE IT WAS!
AND MY HEAD IS KILLING ME!
RELAX. DON'T YOU REMEMBER WHAT SHADOR SAID?
IT'S ALL PART OF HIS PLAN... OR THEIR PLAN...
"TEST THEM, THEN WRECK THEM. YOU'LL SEE."
GUYS? I JUST NOTICED SOME-THING.
MAGNIFICENT COFFEE

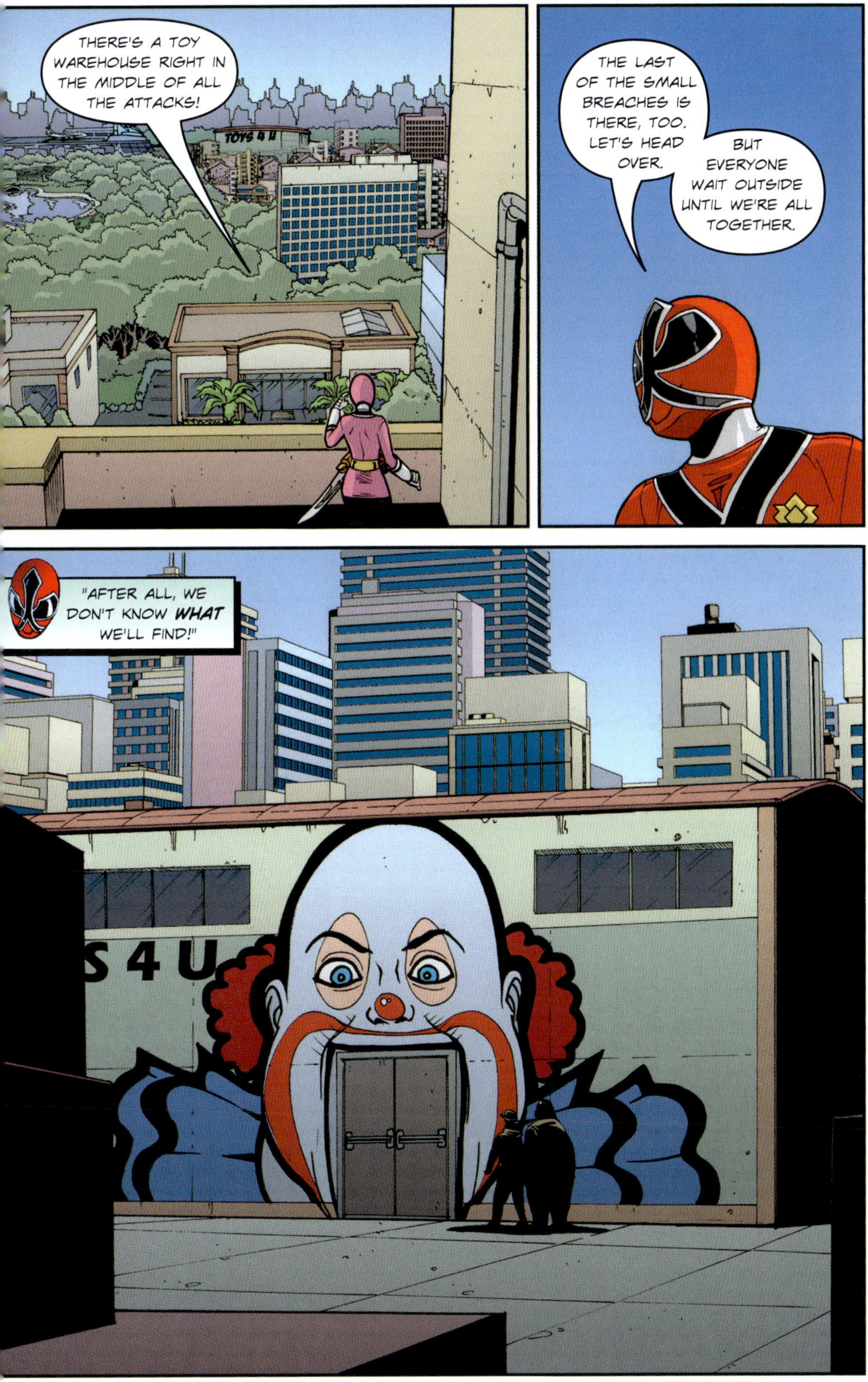
THERE'S A TOY WAREHOUSE RIGHT IN THE MIDDLE OF ALL THE ATTACKS!
TOYS 4 U
THE LAST OF THE SMALL BREACHES IS THERE, TOO. LET'S HEAD OVER.
BUT EVERYONE WAIT OUTSIDE UNTIL WE'RE ALL TOGETHER.
"AFTER ALL, WE DON'T KNOW **WHAT** WE'LL FIND!"
S 4 U

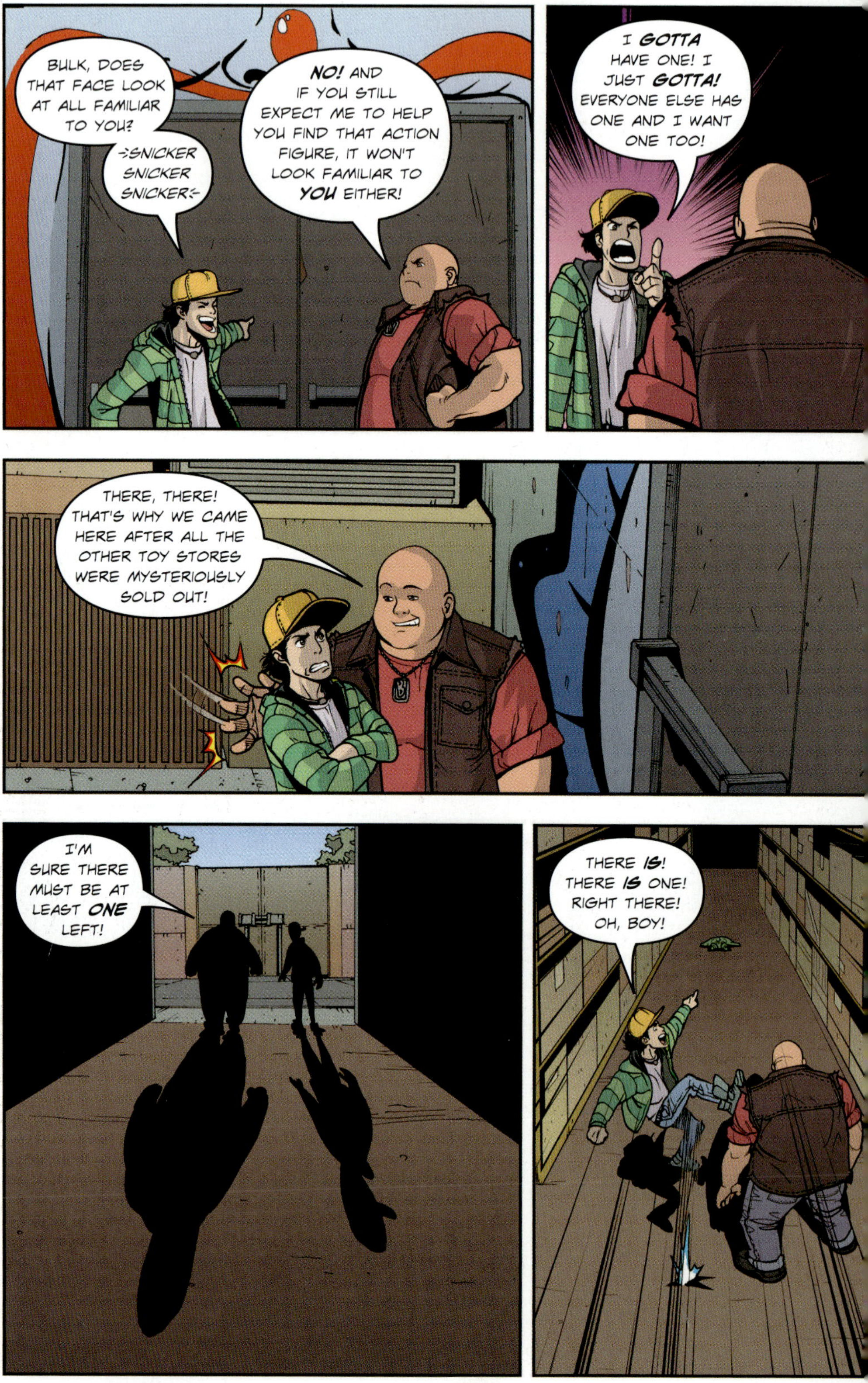
BULK, DOES THAT FACE LOOK AT ALL FAMILIAR TO YOU?
-SNICKER SNICKER SNICKER-
NO! AND IF YOU STILL EXPECT ME TO HELP YOU FIND THAT ACTION FIGURE, IT WON'T LOOK FAMILIAR TO YOU EITHER!
I GOTTA HAVE ONE! I JUST GOTTA! EVERYONE ELSE HAS ONE AND I WANT ONE TOO!
THERE, THERE! THAT'S WHY WE CAME HERE AFTER ALL THE OTHER TOY STORES WERE MYSTERIOUSLY SOLD OUT!
I'M SURE THERE MUST BE AT LEAST ONE LEFT!
THERE IS! THERE IS ONE! RIGHT THERE! OH, BOY!

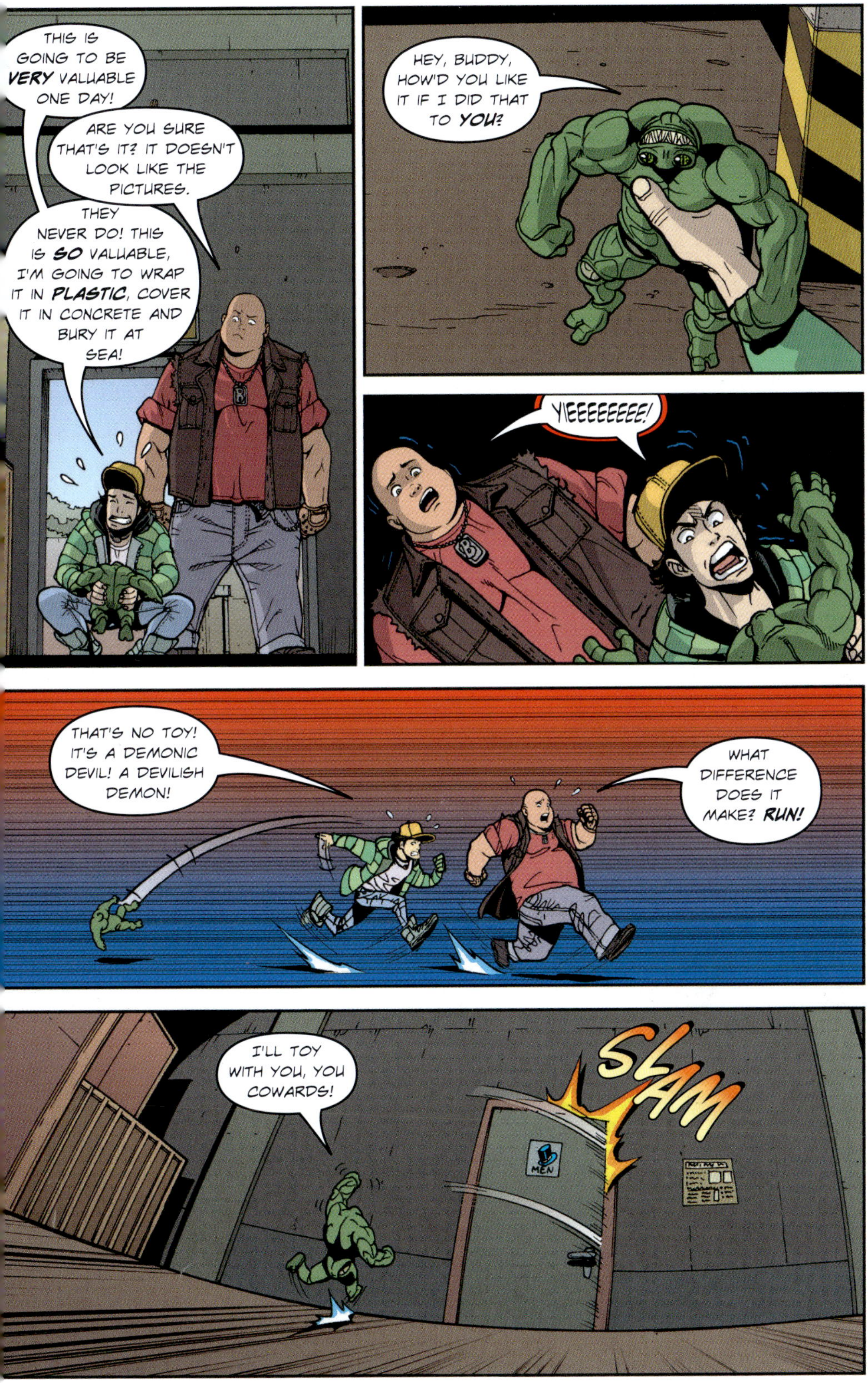
THIS IS GOING TO BE VERY VALUABLE ONE DAY!
ARE YOU SURE THAT'S IT? IT DOESN'T LOOK LIKE THE PICTURES.
THEY NEVER DO! THIS IS SO VALUABLE, I'M GOING TO WRAP IT IN PLASTIC, COVER IT IN CONCRETE AND BURY IT AT SEA!
HEY, BUDDY, HOW'D YOU LIKE IT IF I DID THAT TO YOU?
YIEEEEEEEEE!
THAT'S NO TOY! IT'S A DEMONIC DEVIL! A DEVILISH DEMON!
WHAT DIFFERENCE DOES IT MAKE? RUN!
I'LL TOY WITH YOU, YOU COWARDS!
SLAM
MEN

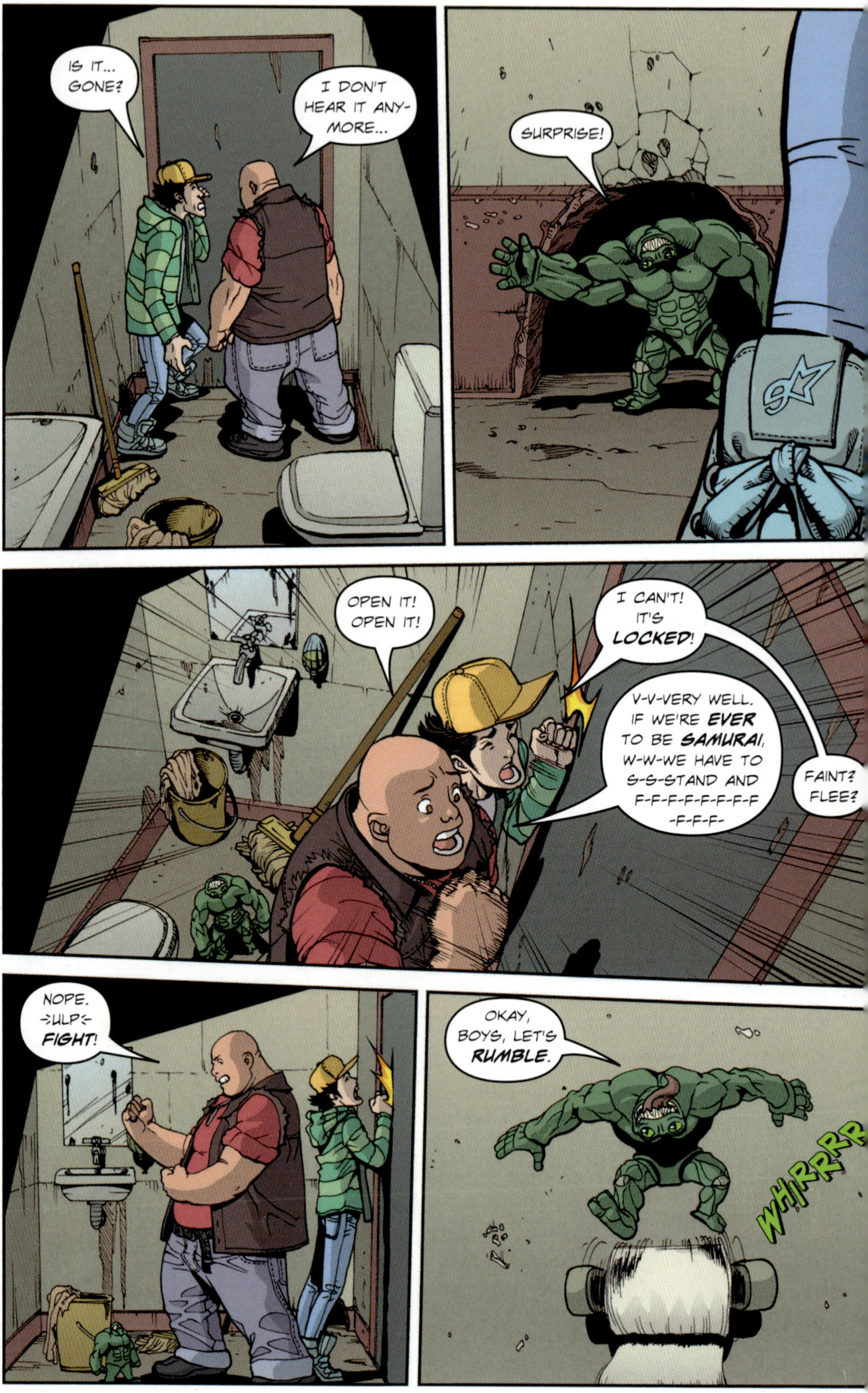
IS IT... GONE?
I DON'T HEAR IT ANY-MORE...
SURPRISE!
OPEN IT! OPEN IT!
I CAN'T! IT'S **LOCKED**!
FAINT? FLEE?
V-V-VERY WELL. IF WE'RE **EVER** TO BE **SAMURAI**, W-W-WE HAVE TO S-S-STAND AND F-F-F-F-F-F-F-F-F -F-F-F-
NOPE. -ULP- **FIGHT**!
OKAY, BOYS, LET'S **RUMBLE**.
WHIRRRR

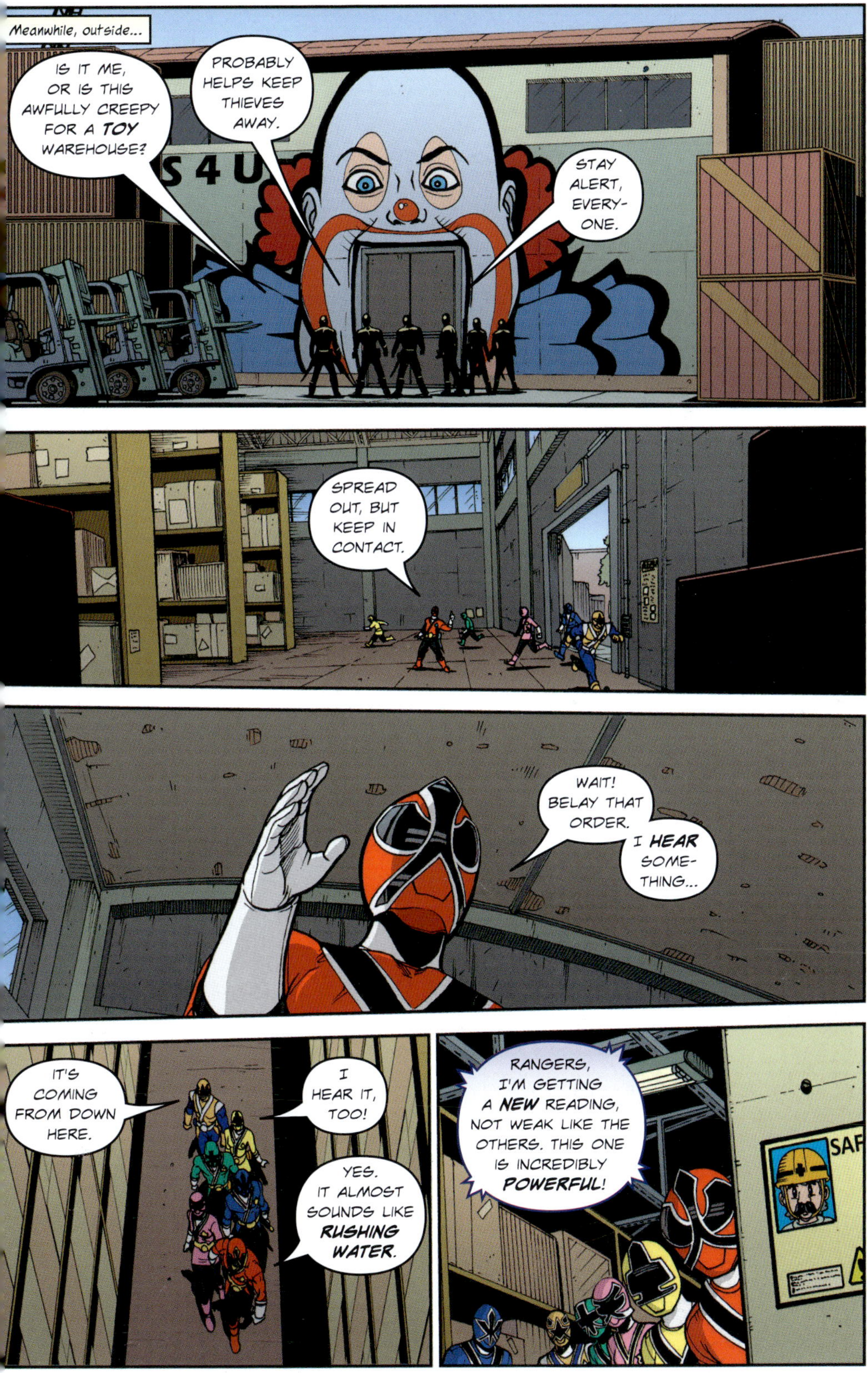
Meanwhile, outside...
IS IT ME, OR IS THIS AWFULLY CREEPY FOR A TOY WAREHOUSE?
PROBABLY HELPS KEEP THIEVES AWAY.
STAY ALERT, EVERY-ONE.
SPREAD OUT, BUT KEEP IN CONTACT.
WAIT! BELAY THAT ORDER.
I HEAR SOME-THING...
IT'S COMING FROM DOWN HERE.
I HEAR IT, TOO!
YES. IT ALMOST SOUNDS LIKE RUSHING WATER.
RANGERS, I'M GETTING A NEW READING, NOT WEAK LIKE THE OTHERS. THIS ONE IS INCREDIBLY POWERFUL!

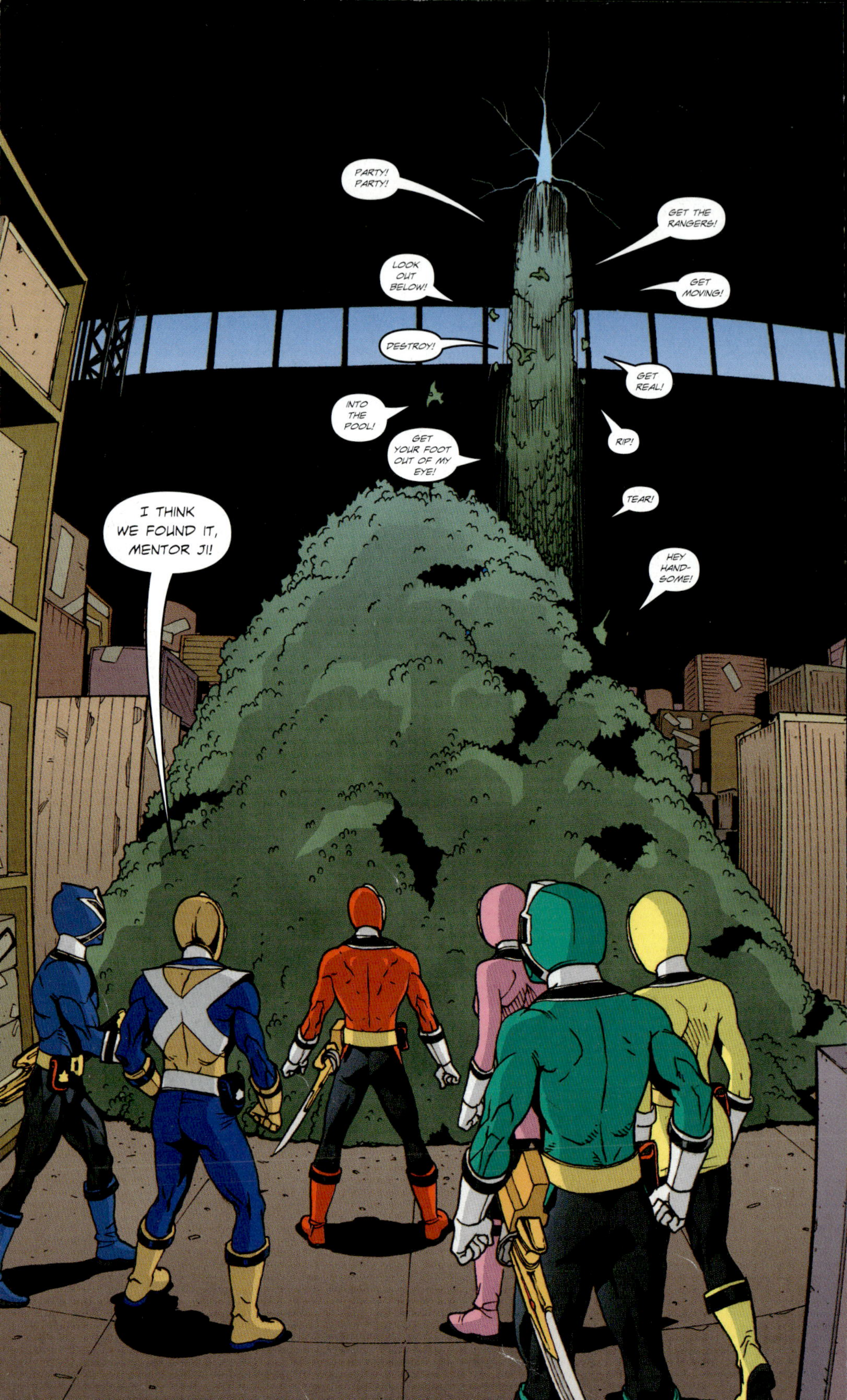
PARTY! PARTY!
GET THE RANGERS!
LOOK OUT BELOW!
GET MOVING!
DESTROY!
GET REAL!
INTO THE POOL!
GET YOUR FOOT OUT OF MY EYE!
RIP!
TEAR!
I THINK WE FOUND IT, MENTOR JI!
HEY HAND-SOME!

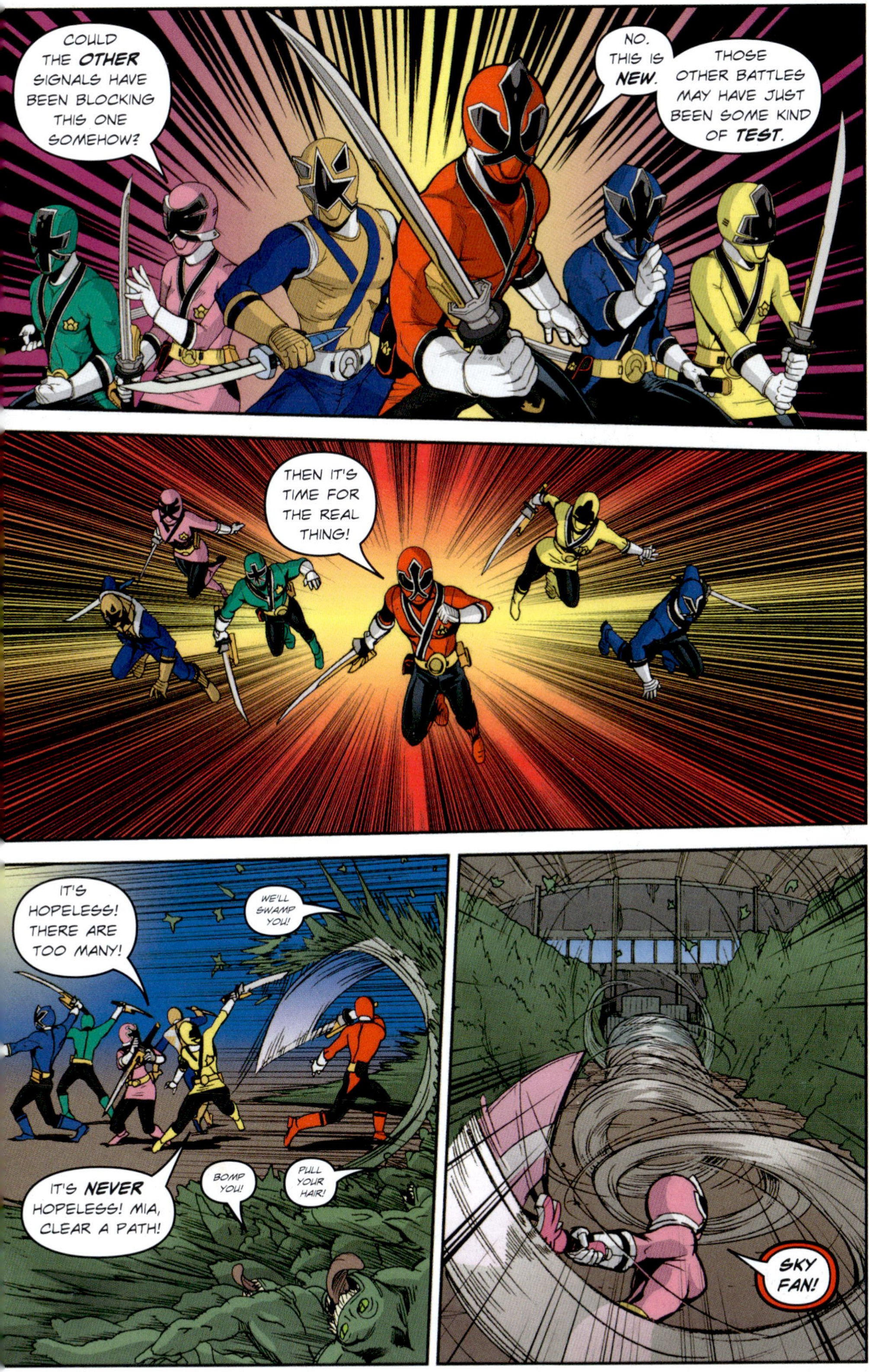
COULD THE OTHER SIGNALS HAVE BEEN BLOCKING THIS ONE SOMEHOW?
NO. THIS IS NEW.
THOSE OTHER BATTLES MAY HAVE JUST BEEN SOME KIND OF TEST.
THEN IT'S TIME FOR THE REAL THING!
IT'S HOPELESS! THERE ARE TOO MANY!
WE'LL SWAMP YOU!
IT'S NEVER HOPELESS! MIA, CLEAR A PATH!
BOMP YOU!
PULL YOUR HAIR!
SKY FAN!

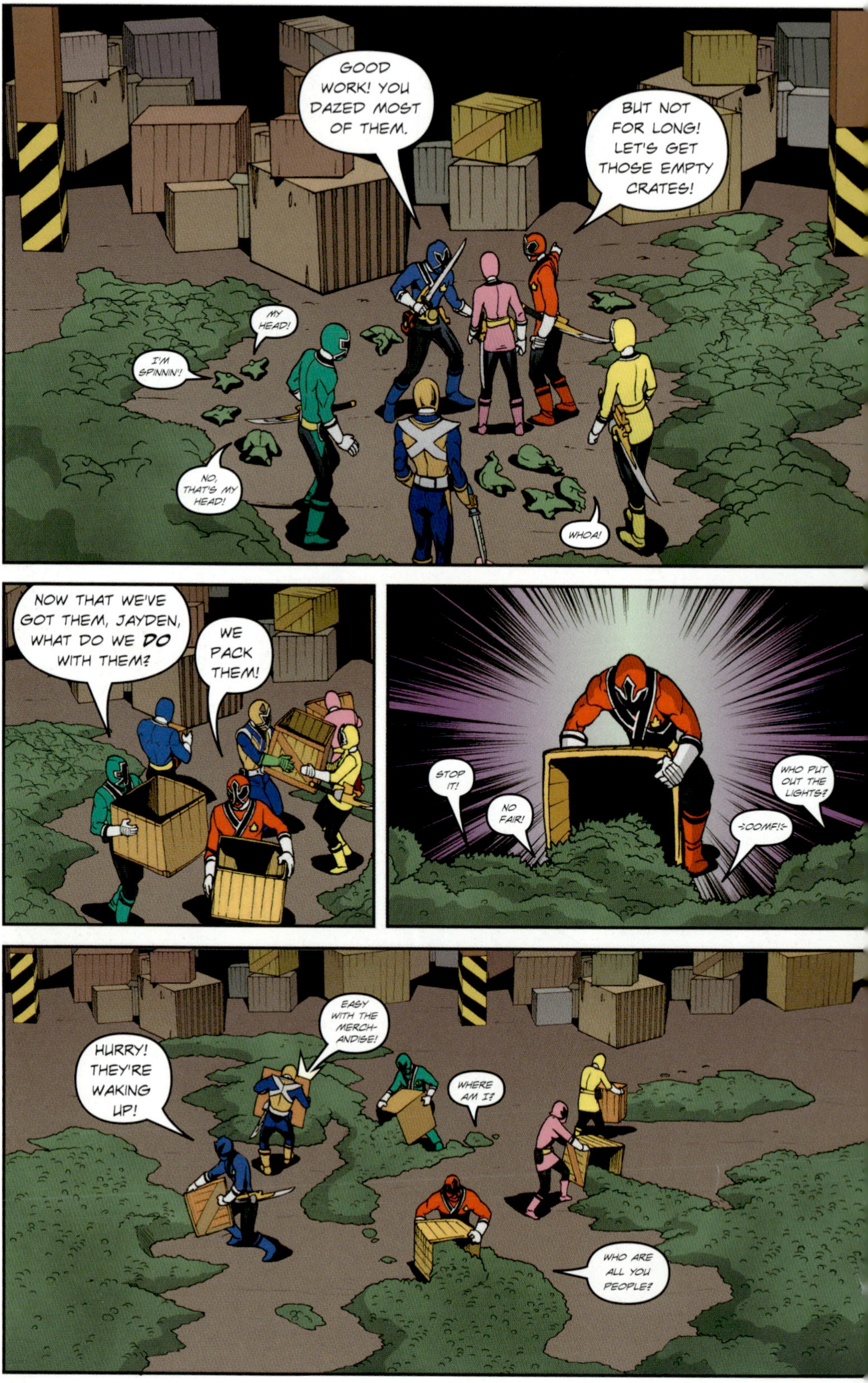
GOOD WORK! YOU DAZED MOST OF THEM.
BUT NOT FOR LONG! LET'S GET THOSE EMPTY CRATES!
MY HEAD!
I'M SPINNIN'!
NO, THAT'S MY HEAD!
WHOA!
NOW THAT WE'VE GOT THEM, JAYDEN, WHAT DO WE DO WITH THEM?
WE PACK THEM!
STOP IT!
NO FAIR!
WHO PUT OUT THE LIGHTS?
>OOMF!<
HURRY! THEY'RE WAKING UP!
EASY WITH THE MERCH-ANDISE!
WHERE AM I?
WHO ARE ALL YOU PEOPLE?

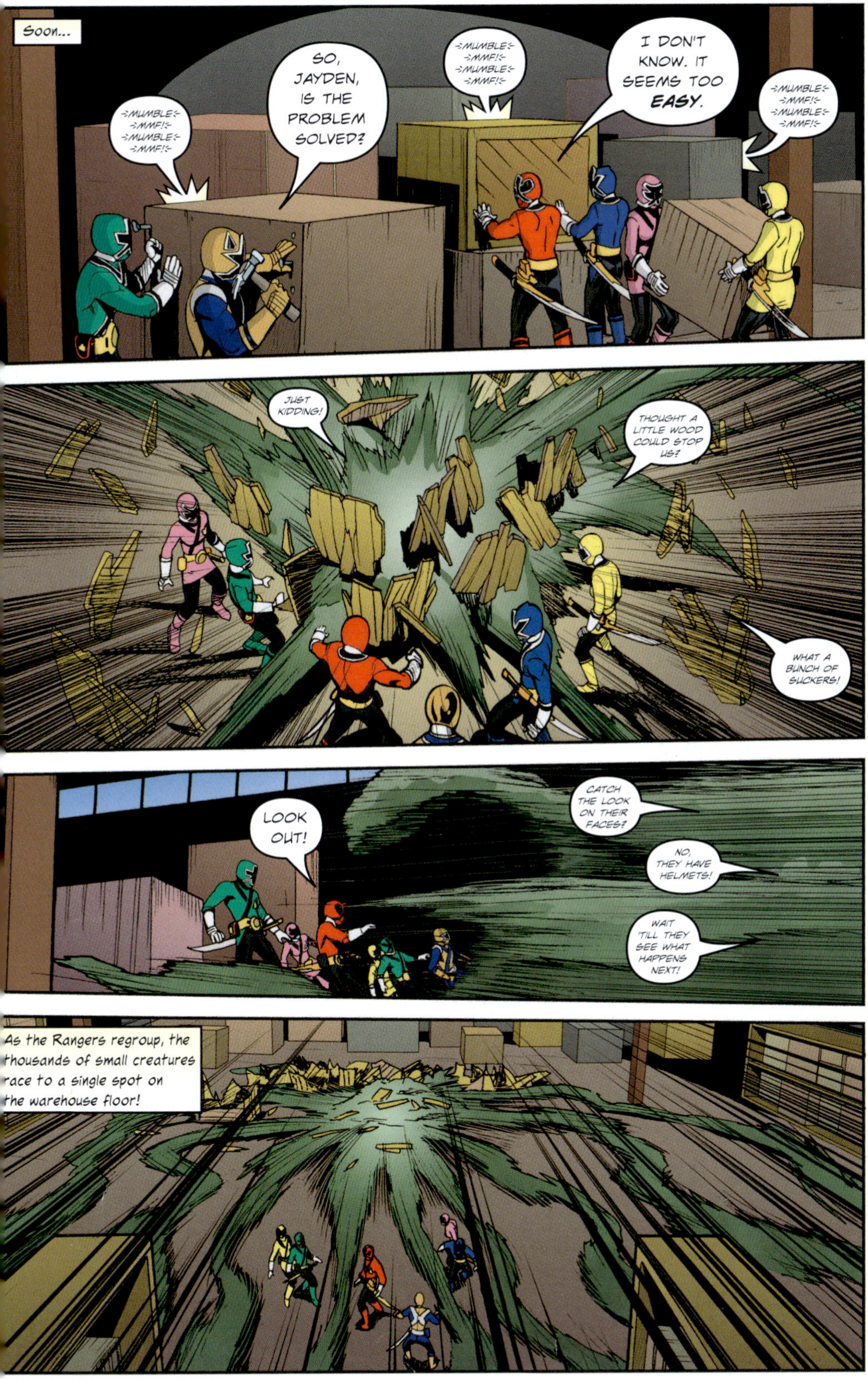
Soon...
-MUMBLE- -MMF!- -MUMBLE- -MMF!-
SO, JAYDEN, IS THE PROBLEM SOLVED?
-MUMBLE- -MMF!- -MUMBLE- -MMF!-
I DON'T KNOW. IT SEEMS TOO EASY.
-MUMBLE- -MMF!- -MUMBLE- -MMF!-
JUST KIDDING!
THOUGHT A LITTLE WOOD COULD STOP US?
WHAT A BUNCH OF SUCKERS!
LOOK OUT!
CATCH THE LOOK ON THEIR FACES?
NO, THEY HAVE HELMETS!
WAIT 'TILL THEY SEE WHAT HAPPENS NEXT!
As the Rangers regroup, the thousands of small creatures race to a single spot on the warehouse floor!

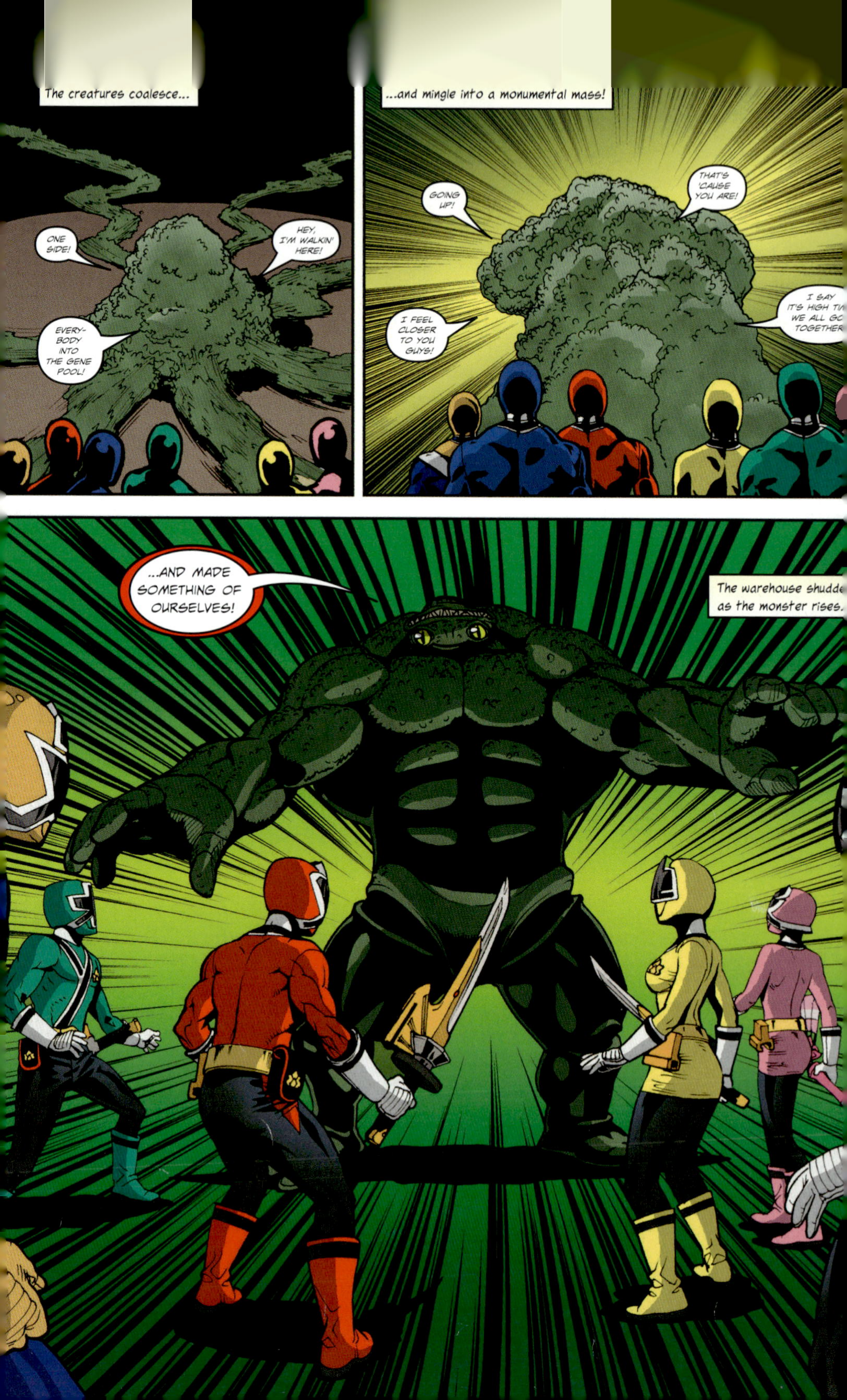
The creatures coalesce...
ONE SIDE!
HEY, I'M WALKIN' HERE!
EVERY-BODY INTO THE GENE POOL!
...and mingle into a monumental mass!
GOING UP!
THAT'S 'CAUSE YOU ARE!
I FEEL CLOSER TO YOU GUYS!
I SAY IT'S HIGH TI WE ALL GO TOGETHER
...AND MADE SOMETHING OF OURSELVES!
The warehouse shudde as the monster rises.

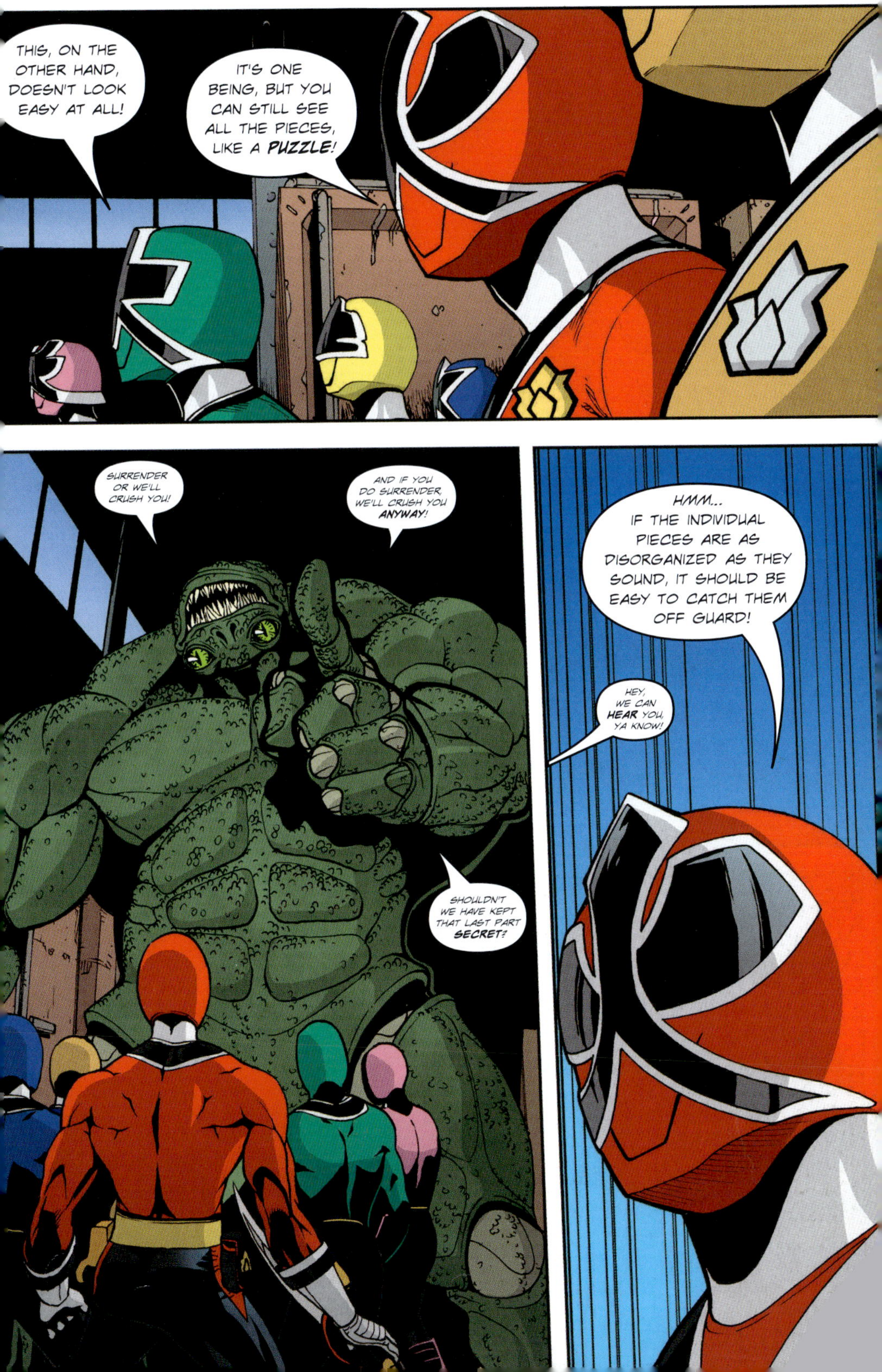
THIS, ON THE OTHER HAND, DOESN'T LOOK EASY AT ALL!
IT'S ONE BEING, BUT YOU CAN STILL SEE ALL THE PIECES, LIKE A PUZZLE!
SURRENDER OR WE'LL CRUSH YOU!
AND IF YOU DO SURRENDER, WE'LL CRUSH YOU ANYWAY!
SHOULDN'T WE HAVE KEPT THAT LAST PART SECRET?
HMM... IF THE INDIVIDUAL PIECES ARE AS DISORGANIZED AS THEY SOUND, IT SHOULD BE EASY TO CATCH THEM OFF GUARD!
HEY, WE CAN HEAR YOU, YA KNOW!

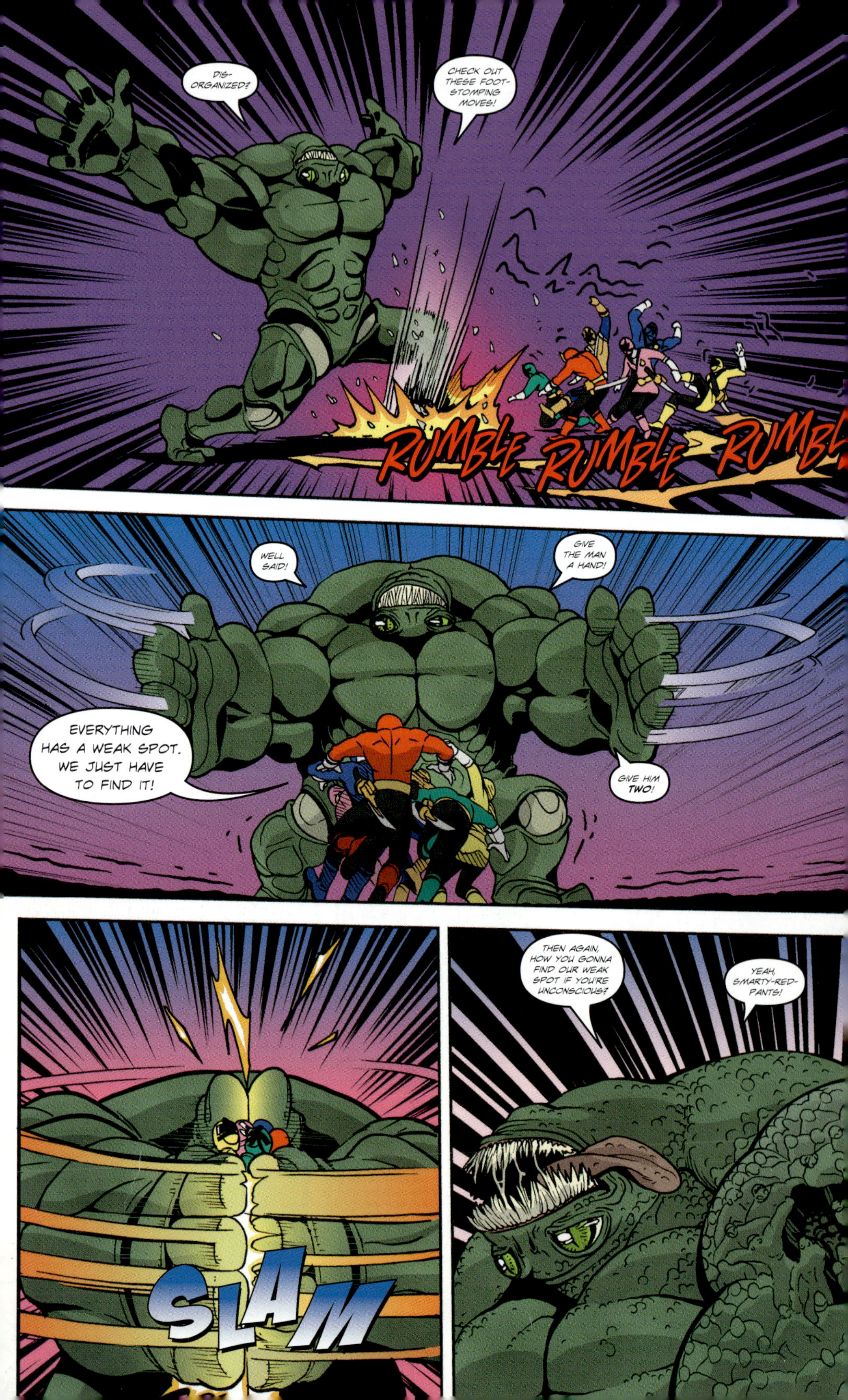

DIS-ORGANIZED?
CHECK OUT THESE FOOT-STOMPING MOVES!
RUMBLE RUMBLE RUMBLE
WELL SAID!
GIVE THE MAN A HAND!
EVERYTHING HAS A WEAK SPOT. WE JUST HAVE TO FIND IT!
GIVE HIM TWO!
SLAM
THEN AGAIN, HOW YOU GONNA FIND OUR WEAK SPOT IF YOU'RE UNCONSCIOUS?
YEAH, SMARTY-RED-PANTS!

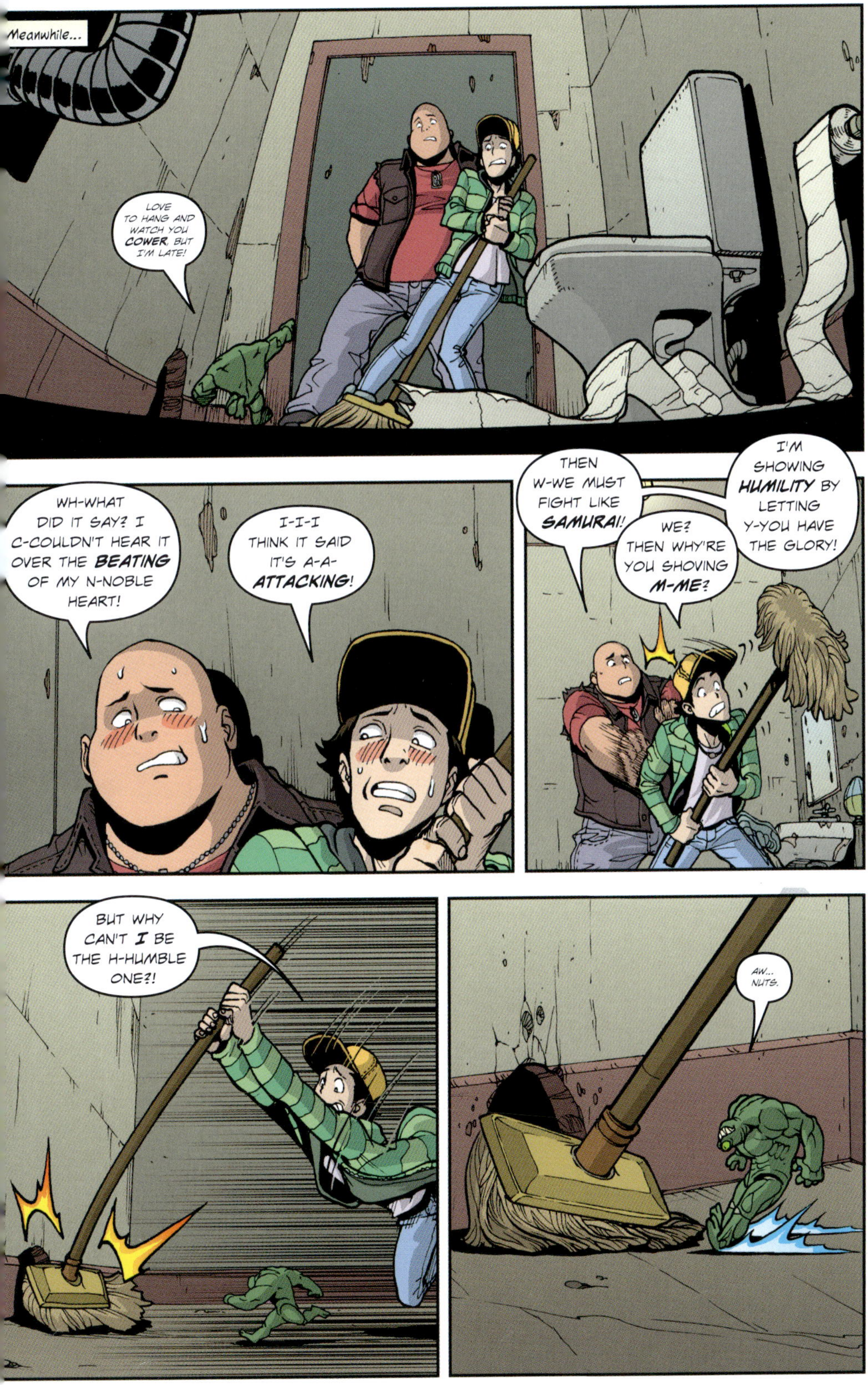
Meanwhile...
LOVE TO HANG AND WATCH YOU COWER, BUT I'M LATE!
WH-WHAT DID IT SAY? I C-COULDN'T HEAR IT OVER THE BEATING OF MY N-NOBLE HEART!
I-I-I THINK IT SAID IT'S A-A-ATTACKING!
THEN W-WE MUST FIGHT LIKE SAMURAI!
I'M SHOWING HUMILITY BY LETTING Y-YOU HAVE THE GLORY!
WE? THEN WHY'RE YOU SHOVING M-ME?
BUT WHY CAN'T I BE THE H-HUMBLE ONE?!
AW... NUTS.

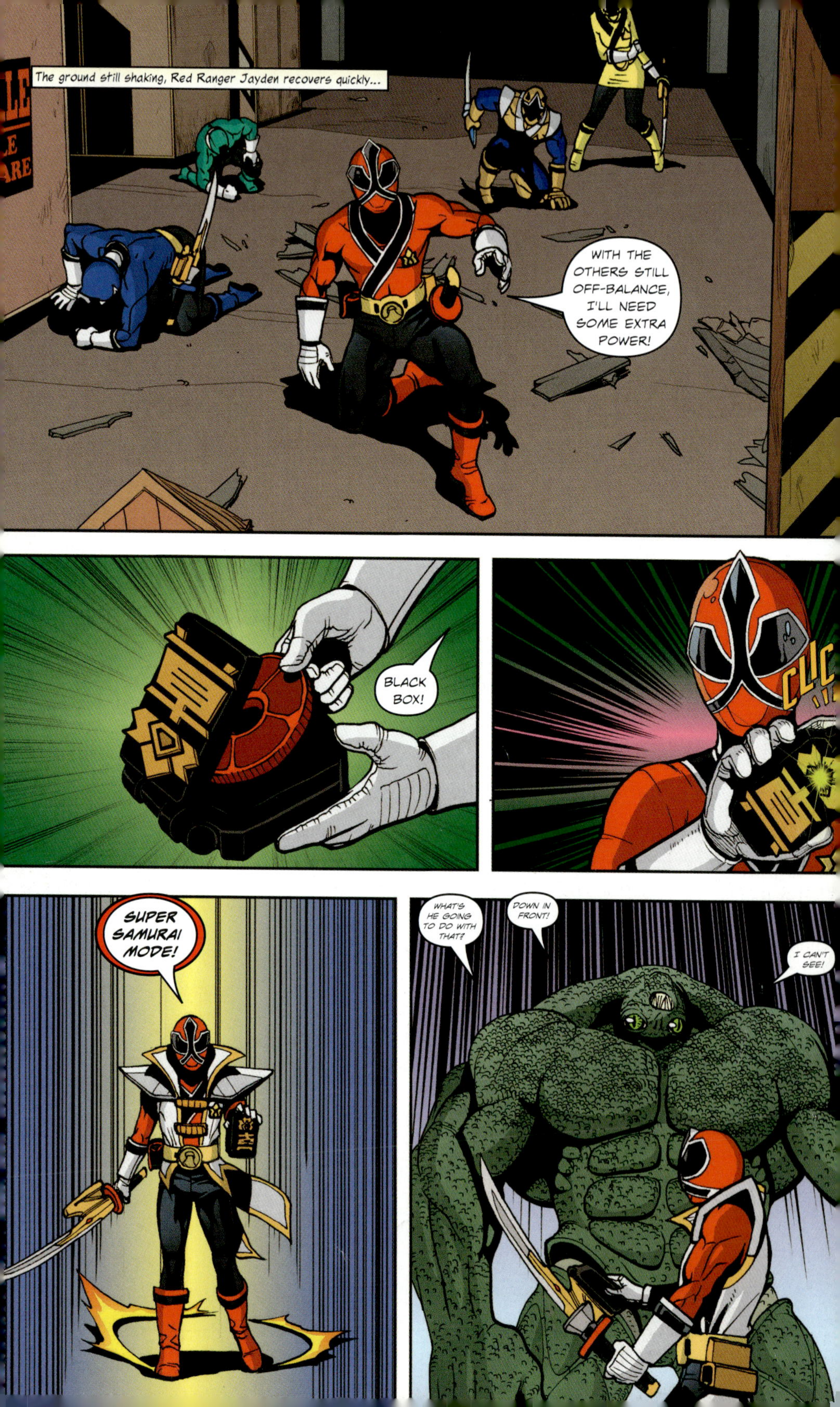
The ground still shaking, Red Ranger Jayden recovers quickly...
WITH THE OTHERS STILL OFF-BALANCE, I'LL NEED SOME EXTRA POWER!
BLACK BOX!
SUPER SAMURAI MODE!
WHAT'S HE GOING TO DO WITH THAT?
DOWN IN FRONT!
I CAN'T SEE!

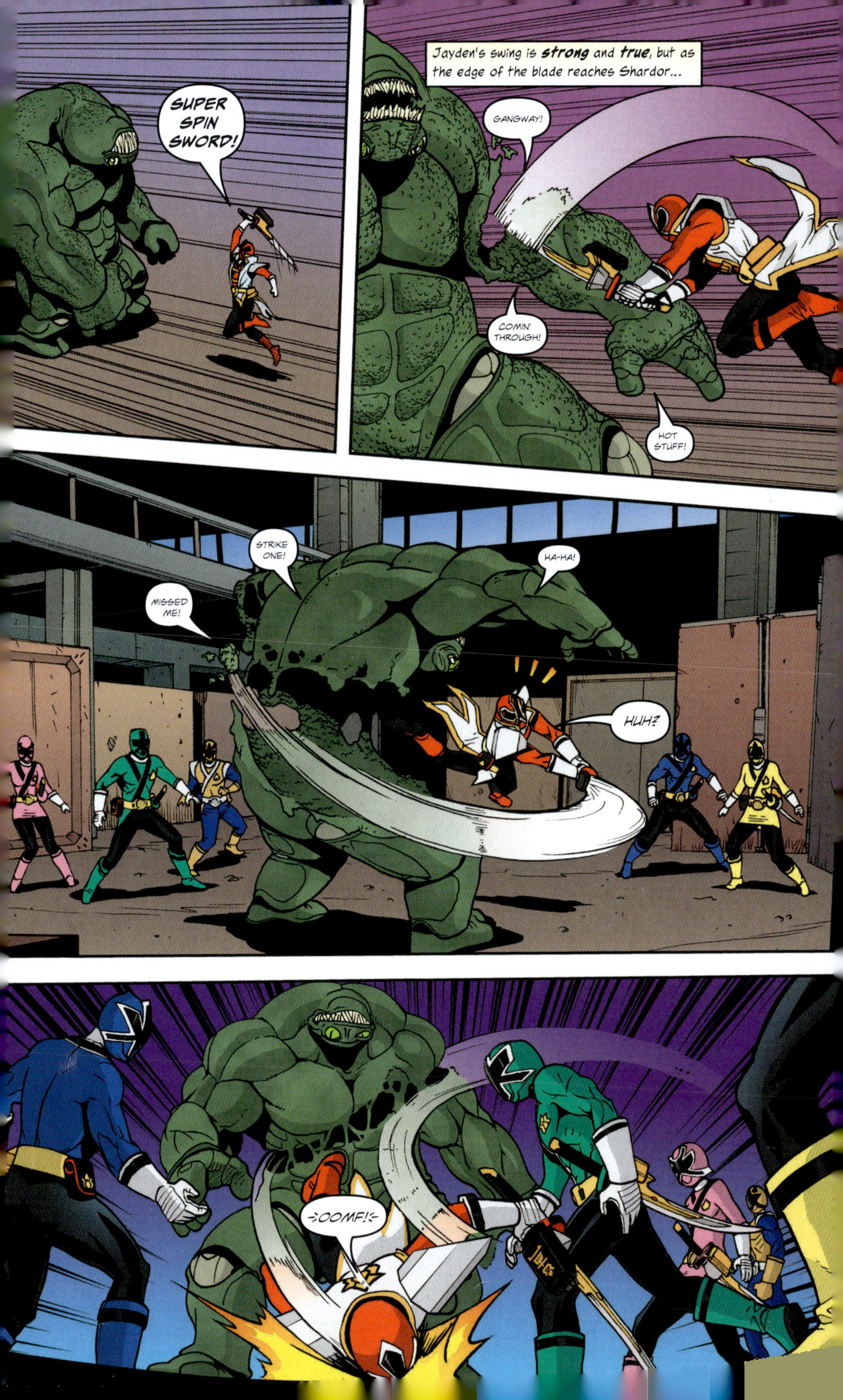
SUPER SPIN SWORD!
Jayden's swing is **strong** and **true**, but as the edge of the blade reaches Shardor...
GANGWAY!
COMIN' THROUGH!
HOT STUFF!
STRIKE ONE!
HA-HA!
MISSED ME!
HUH?
OOMF!

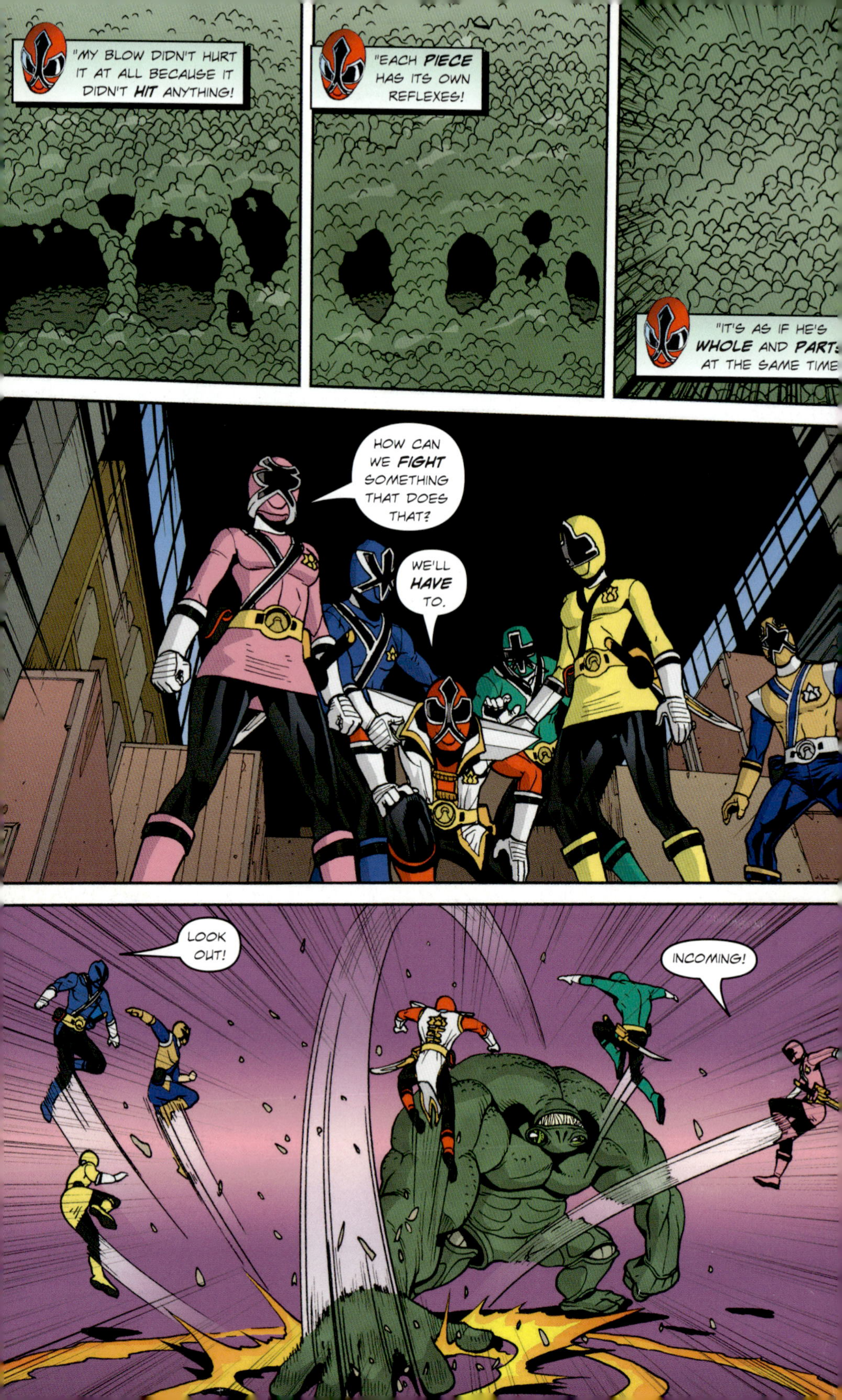
"MY BLOW DIDN'T HURT IT AT ALL BECAUSE IT DIDN'T HIT ANYTHING!
"EACH PIECE HAS ITS OWN REFLEXES!
"IT'S AS IF HE'S WHOLE AND PARTS AT THE SAME TIME
HOW CAN WE FIGHT SOMETHING THAT DOES THAT?
WE'LL HAVE TO.
LOOK OUT!
INCOMING!

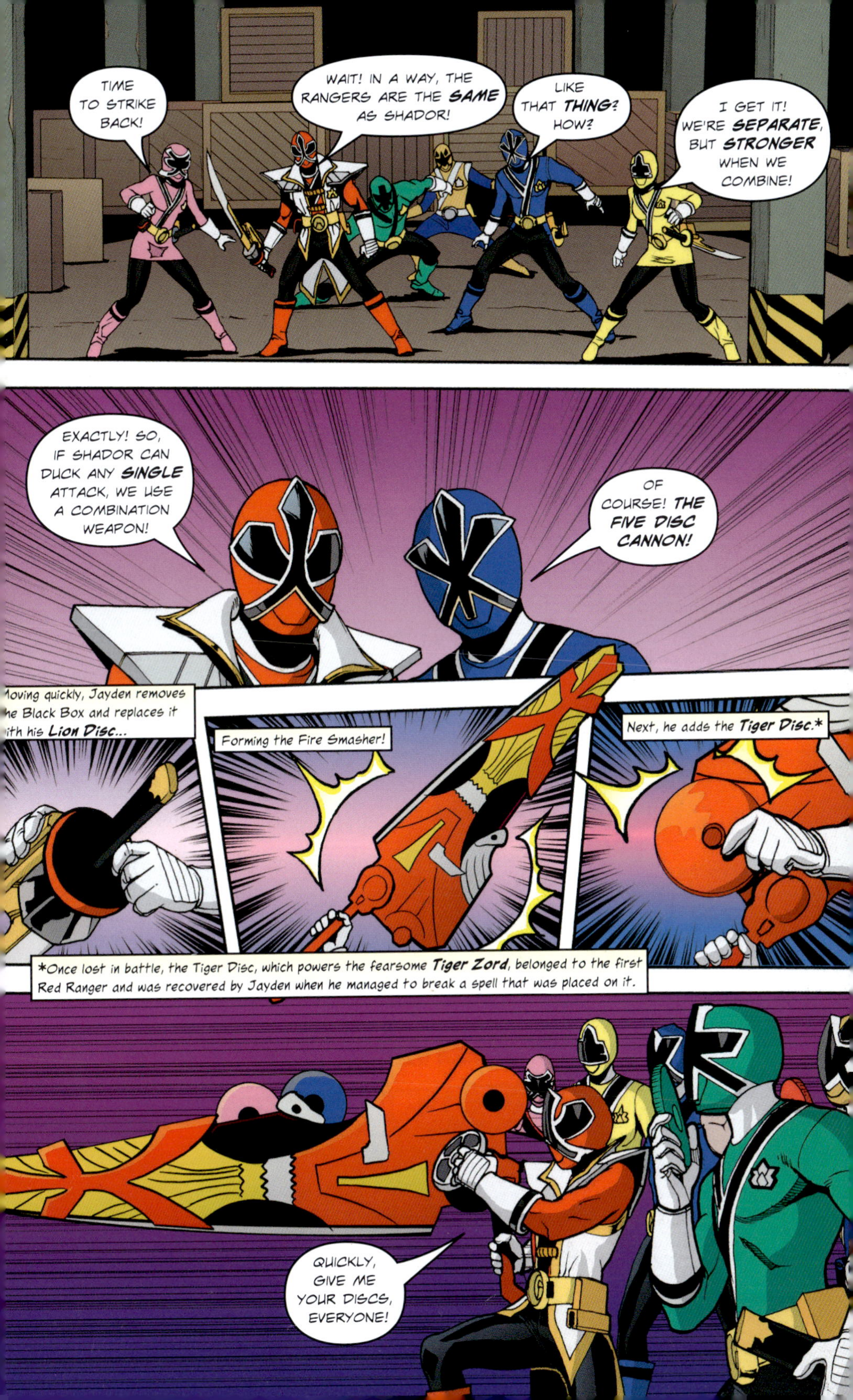
TIME TO STRIKE BACK!
WAIT! IN A WAY, THE RANGERS ARE THE SAME AS SHADOR!
LIKE THAT THING? HOW?
I GET IT! WE'RE SEPARATE, BUT STRONGER WHEN WE COMBINE!
EXACTLY! SO, IF SHADOR CAN DUCK ANY SINGLE ATTACK, WE USE A COMBINATION WEAPON!
OF COURSE! THE FIVE DISC CANNON!
oving quickly, Jayden removes he Black Box and replaces it ith his Lion Disc...
Forming the Fire Smasher!
Next, he adds the Tiger Disc.*
*Once lost in battle, the Tiger Disc, which powers the fearsome Tiger Zord, belonged to the first Red Ranger and was recovered by Jayden when he managed to break a spell that was placed on it.
QUICKLY, GIVE ME YOUR DISCS, EVERYONE!

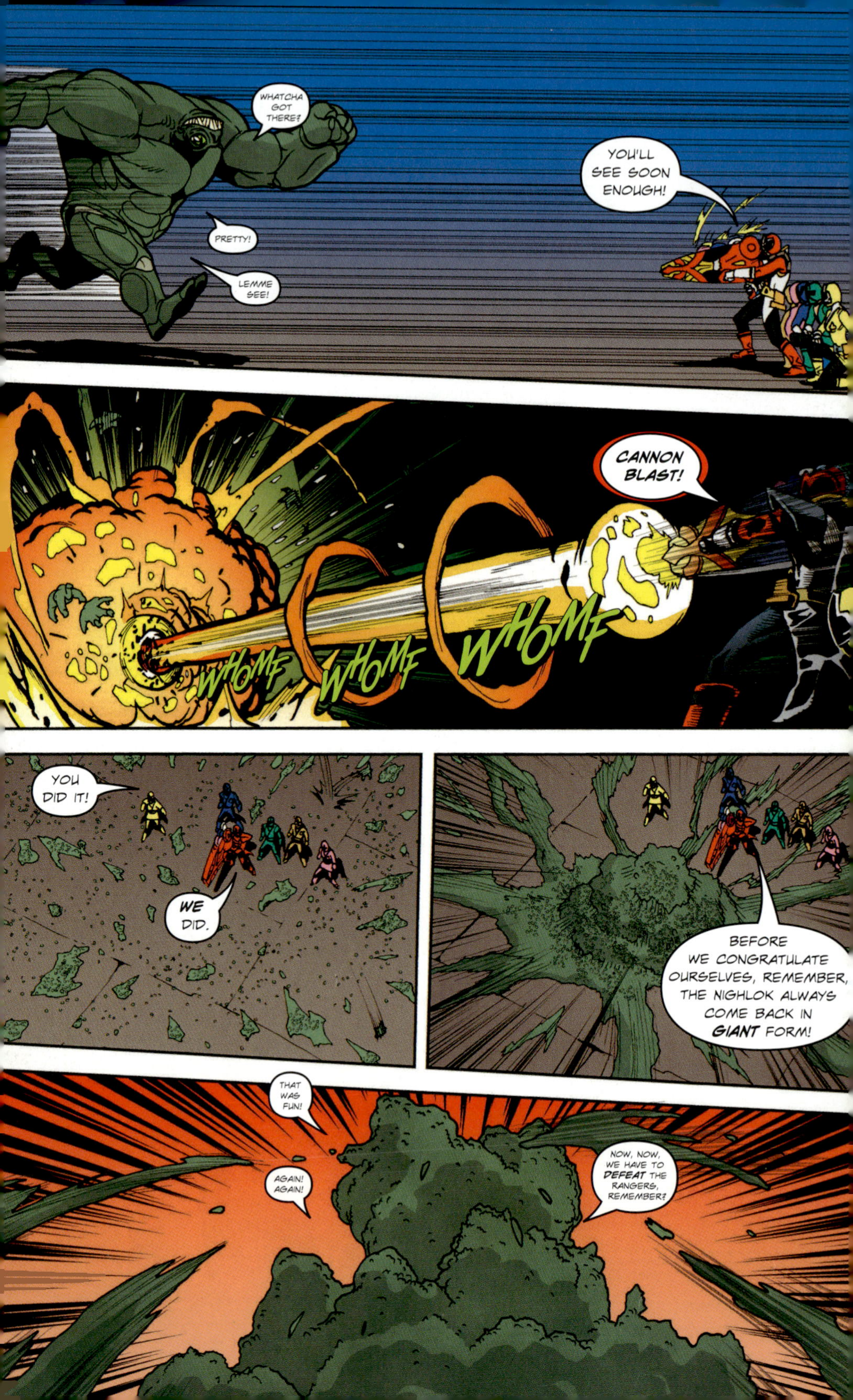
WHATCHA GOT THERE?
PRETTY!
LEMME SEE!
YOU'LL SEE SOON ENOUGH!
CANNON BLAST!
WHOMF WHOMF WHOMF
YOU DID IT!
WE DID.
BEFORE WE CONGRATULATE OURSELVES, REMEMBER, THE NIGHLOK ALWAYS COME BACK IN GIANT FORM!
THAT WAS FUN!
AGAIN! AGAIN!
NOW, NOW, WE HAVE TO DEFEAT THE RANGERS, REMEMBER?

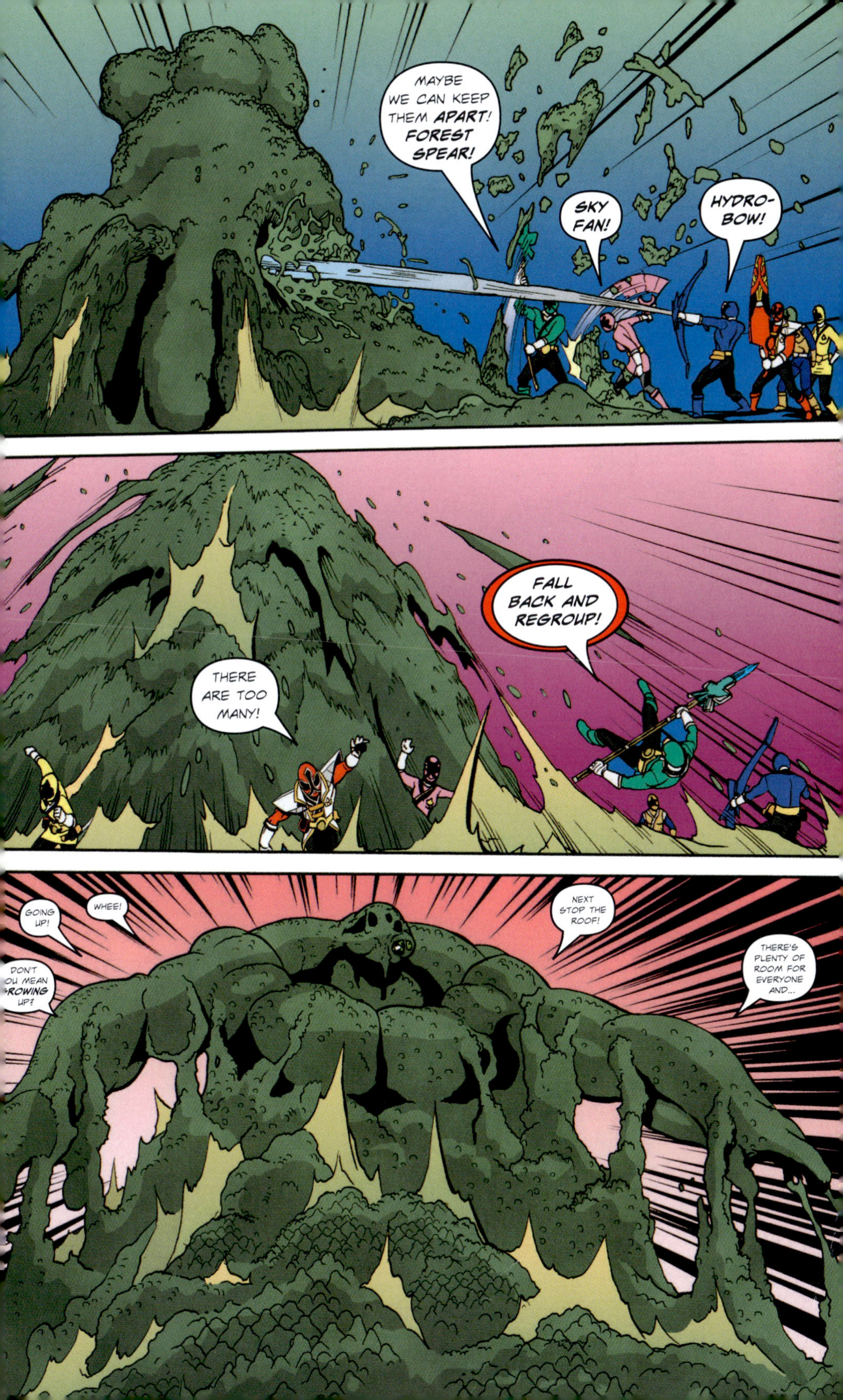
MAYBE WE CAN KEEP THEM APART! FOREST SPEAR!
SKY FAN!
HYDRO-BOW!
FALL BACK AND REGROUP!
THERE ARE TOO MANY!
GOING UP!
WHEE!
DON'T OU MEAN ROWING UP?
NEXT STOP THE ROOF!
THERE'S PLENTY OF ROOM FOR EVERYONE AND...

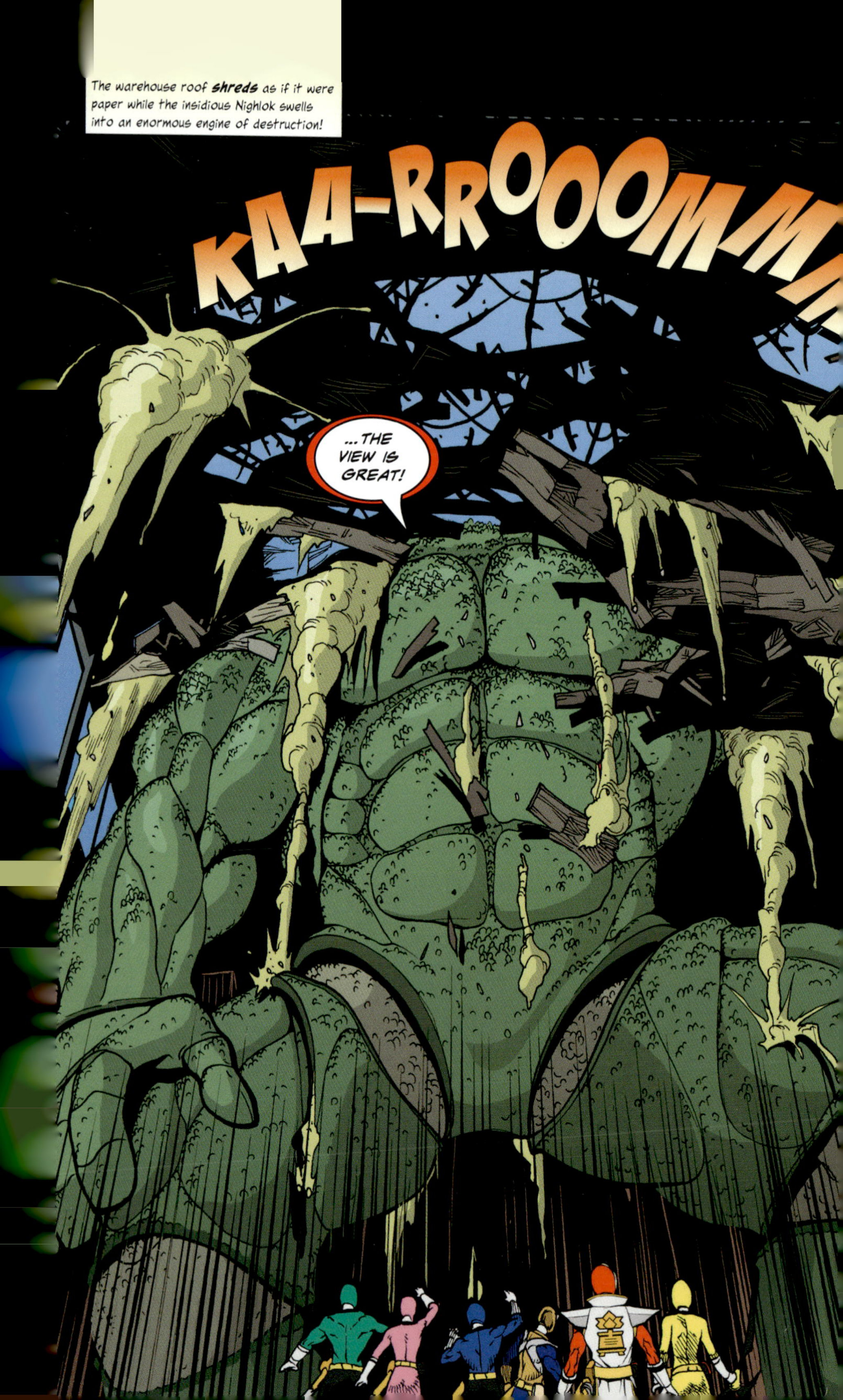
The warehouse roof **shreds** as if it were paper while the insidious Nighlok swells into an enormous engine of destruction!
KAA-RROOOOM-M
...THE VIEW IS GREAT!

The creature turns greedily toward the peaceful city, eager to spread the *terror* and *misery* that will fill the *Sanzu River!*

SO LITTLE TIME, SO MUCH TO *DESTROY!*

Little do the hapless occupants within realize that the shadow on their windows is *more* than a cloudy day!

C'MERE, YOU BIG WACKY!

YOU MAY NOT LIKE IT, BUT YOU'RE GONNA GET A BIG *HUG!*

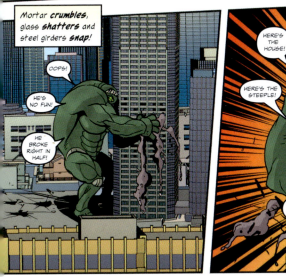

Mortar *crumbles*, glass *shatters* and steel girders *snap!*

OOPS!

HE'S NO FUN!

HE BROKE RIGHT IN HALF!

HERE'S THE HOUSE!

HERE'S THE STEEPLE!

CRACK IT IN HALF!

AND HERE ARE THE *PEOPLE!*

AIEEEE!

HELP US, SOME-ONE!

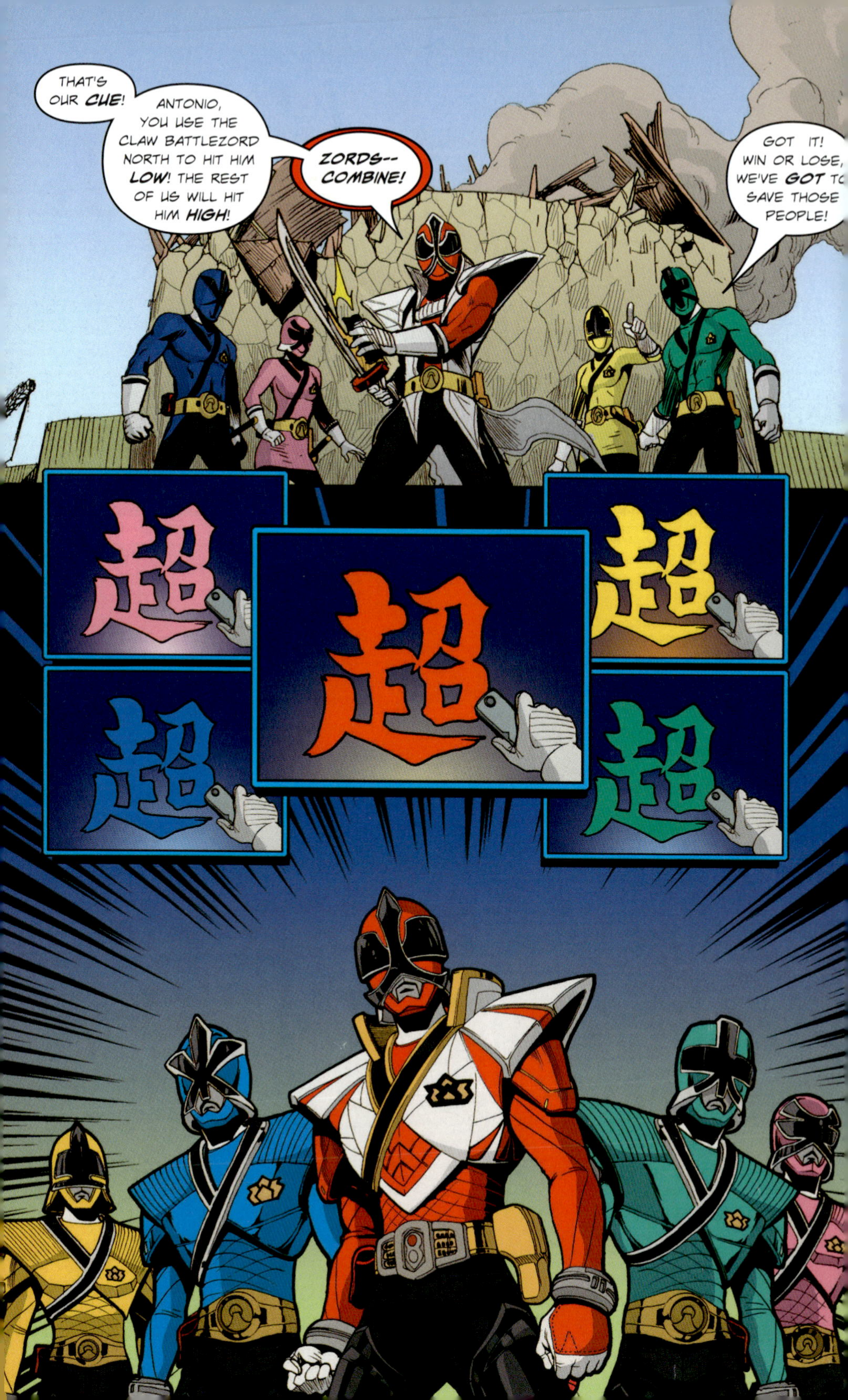
THAT'S OUR CUE!
ANTONIO, YOU USE THE CLAW BATTLEZORD NORTH TO HIT HIM LOW! THE REST OF US WILL HIT HIM HIGH!
ZORDS-- COMBINE!
GOT IT! WIN OR LOSE, WE'VE GOT TO SAVE THOSE PEOPLE!
超
超
超
超
超

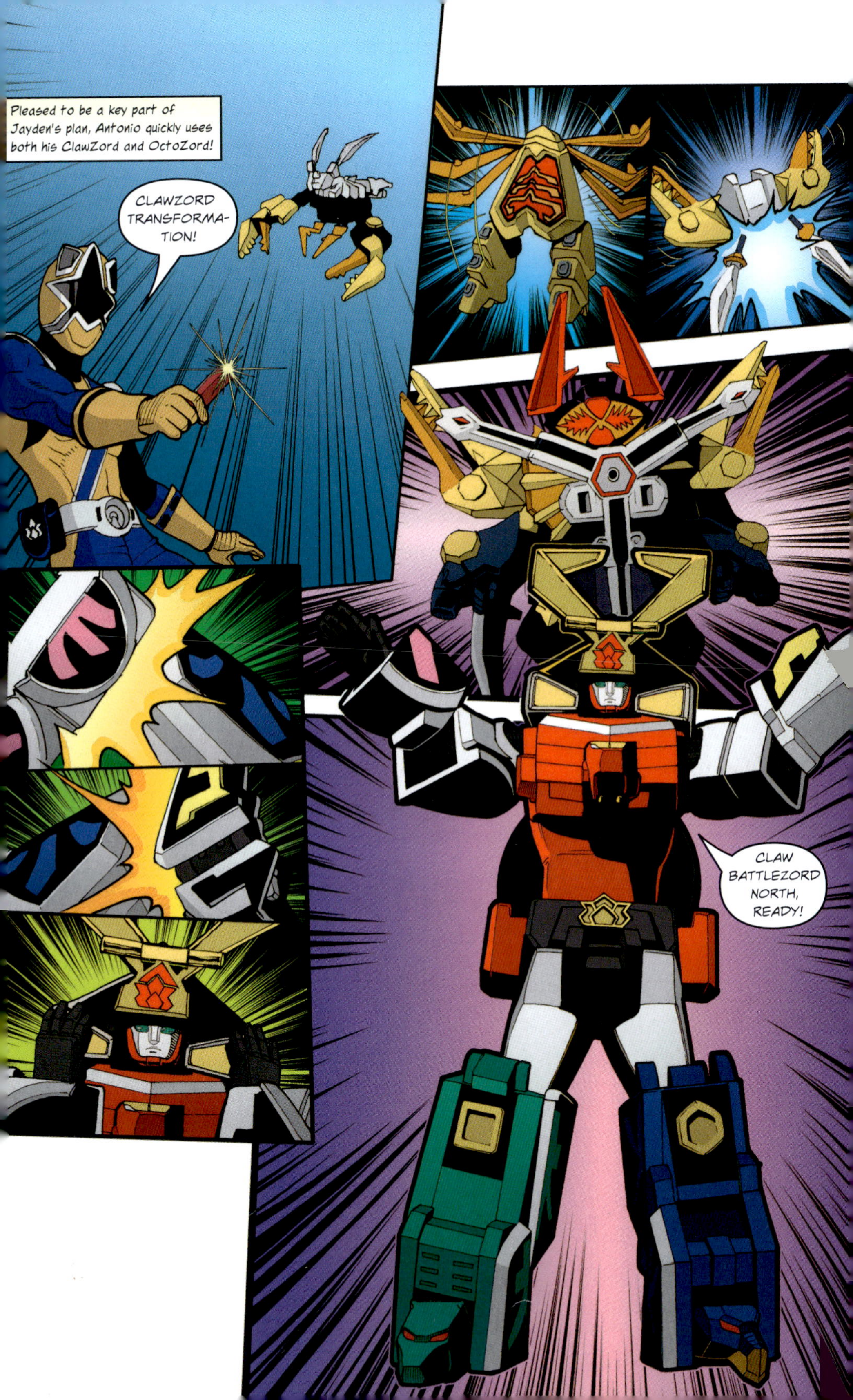
Pleased to be a key part of Jayden's plan, Antonio quickly uses both his ClawZord and OctoZord!
CLAWZORD TRANSFORMA-TION!
CLAW BATTLEZORD NORTH, READY!

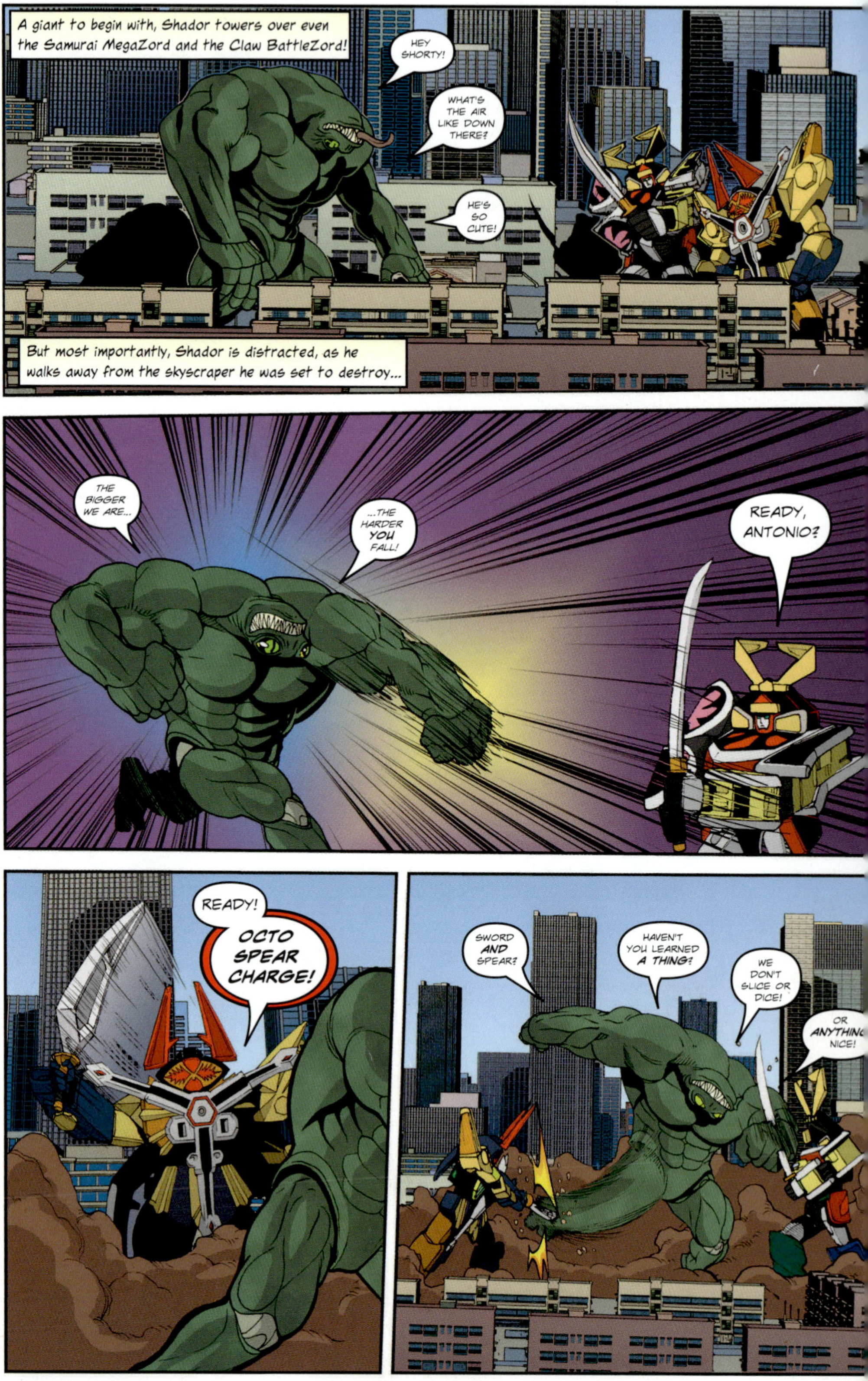
A giant to begin with, Shador towers over even the Samurai MegaZord and the Claw BattleZord!
HEY SHORTY!
WHAT'S THE AIR LIKE DOWN THERE?
HE'S SO CUTE!
But most importantly, Shador is distracted, as he walks away from the skyscraper he was set to destroy...
THE BIGGER WE ARE...
...THE HARDER YOU FALL!
READY, ANTONIO?
READY!
OCTO SPEAR CHARGE!
SWORD AND SPEAR?
HAVEN'T YOU LEARNED A THING?
WE DON'T SLICE OR DICE!
OR ANYTHIN
NICE!

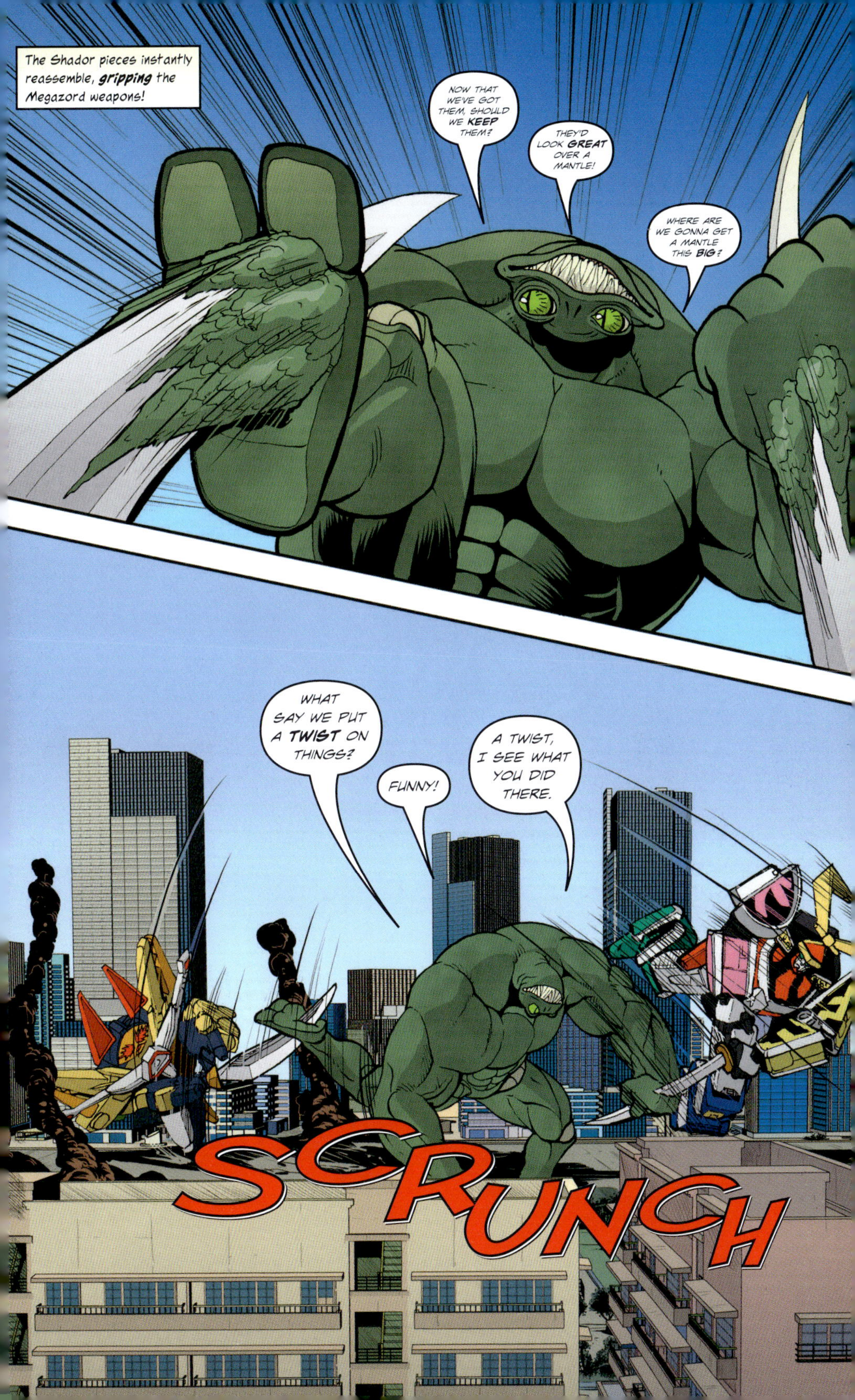
The Shador pieces instantly reassemble, **gripping** the Megazord weapons!
NOW THAT WE'VE GOT THEM, SHOULD WE **KEEP** THEM?
THEY'D LOOK **GREAT** OVER A MANTLE!
WHERE ARE WE GONNA GET A MANTLE THIS **BIG**?
WHAT SAY WE PUT A **TWIST** ON THINGS?
FUNNY!
A TWIST, I SEE WHAT YOU DID THERE.
SCRUNCH

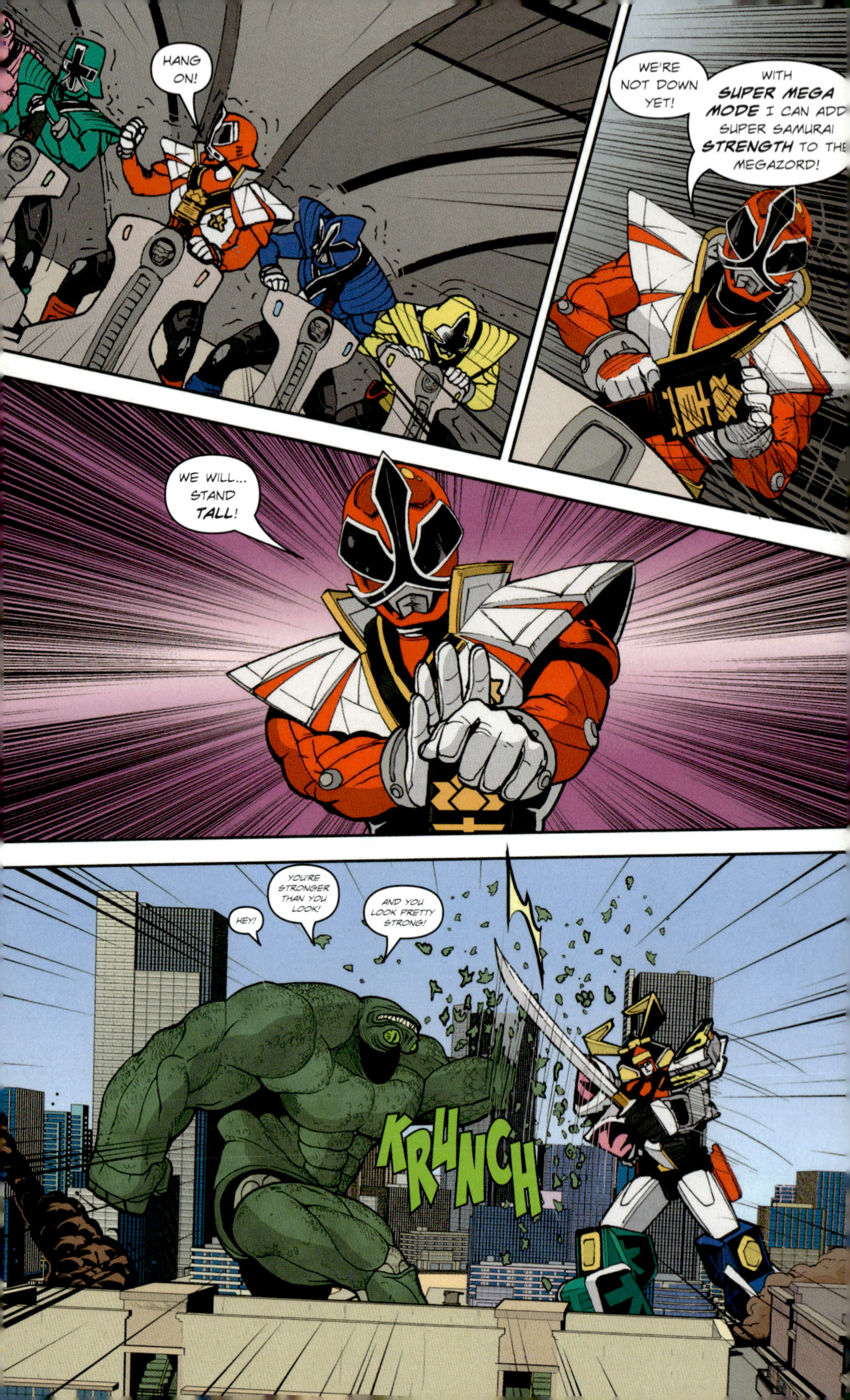
HANG ON!
WE'RE NOT DOWN YET!
WITH SUPER MEGA MODE I CAN ADD SUPER SAMURAI STRENGTH TO THE MEGAZORD!
WE WILL... STAND TALL!
HEY!
YOU'RE STRONGER THAN YOU LOOK!
AND YOU LOOK PRETTY STRONG!
KRUNCH

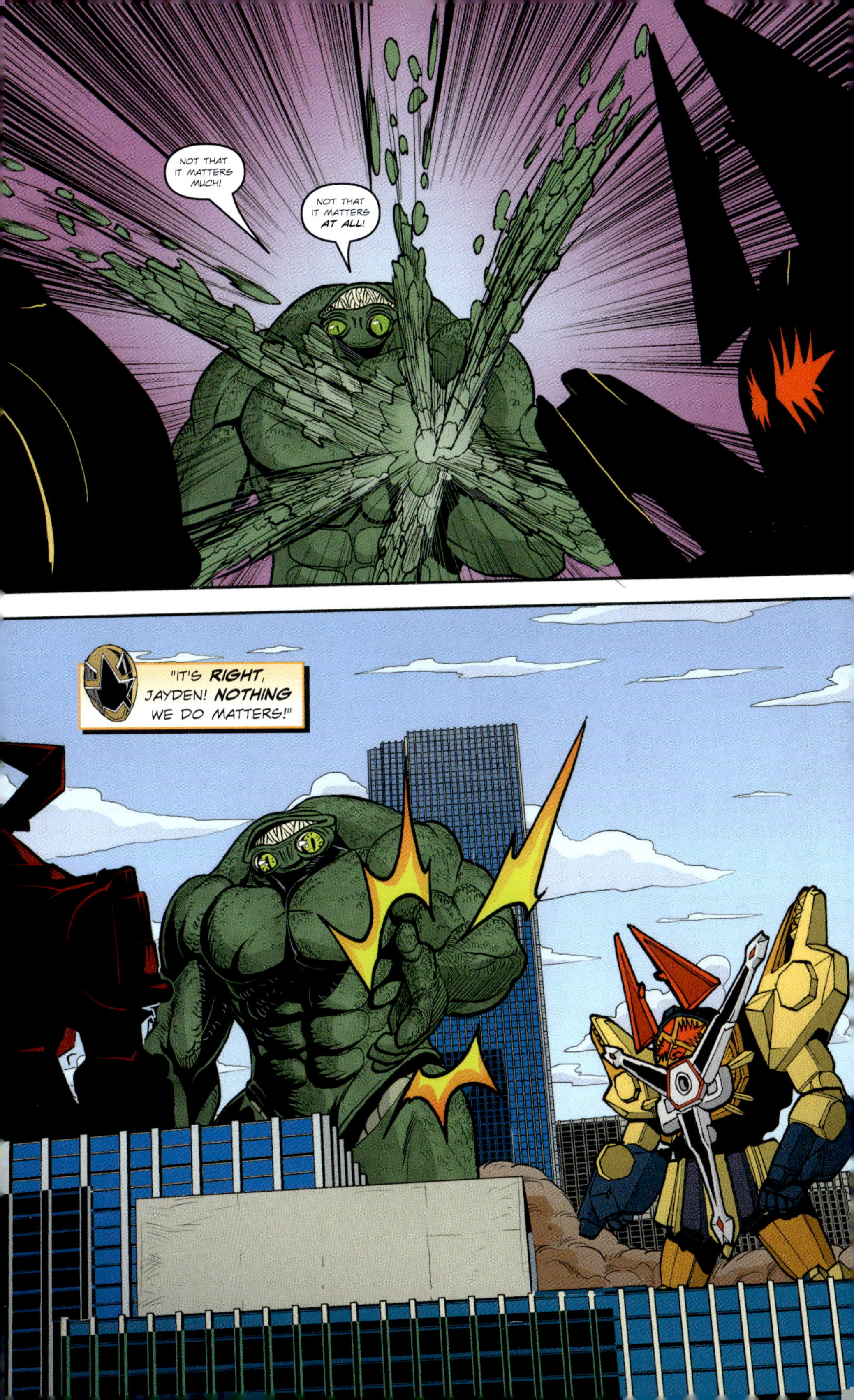
NOT THAT IT MATTERS MUCH!
NOT THAT IT MATTERS AT ALL!
"IT'S RIGHT, JAYDEN! NOTHING WE DO MATTERS!"

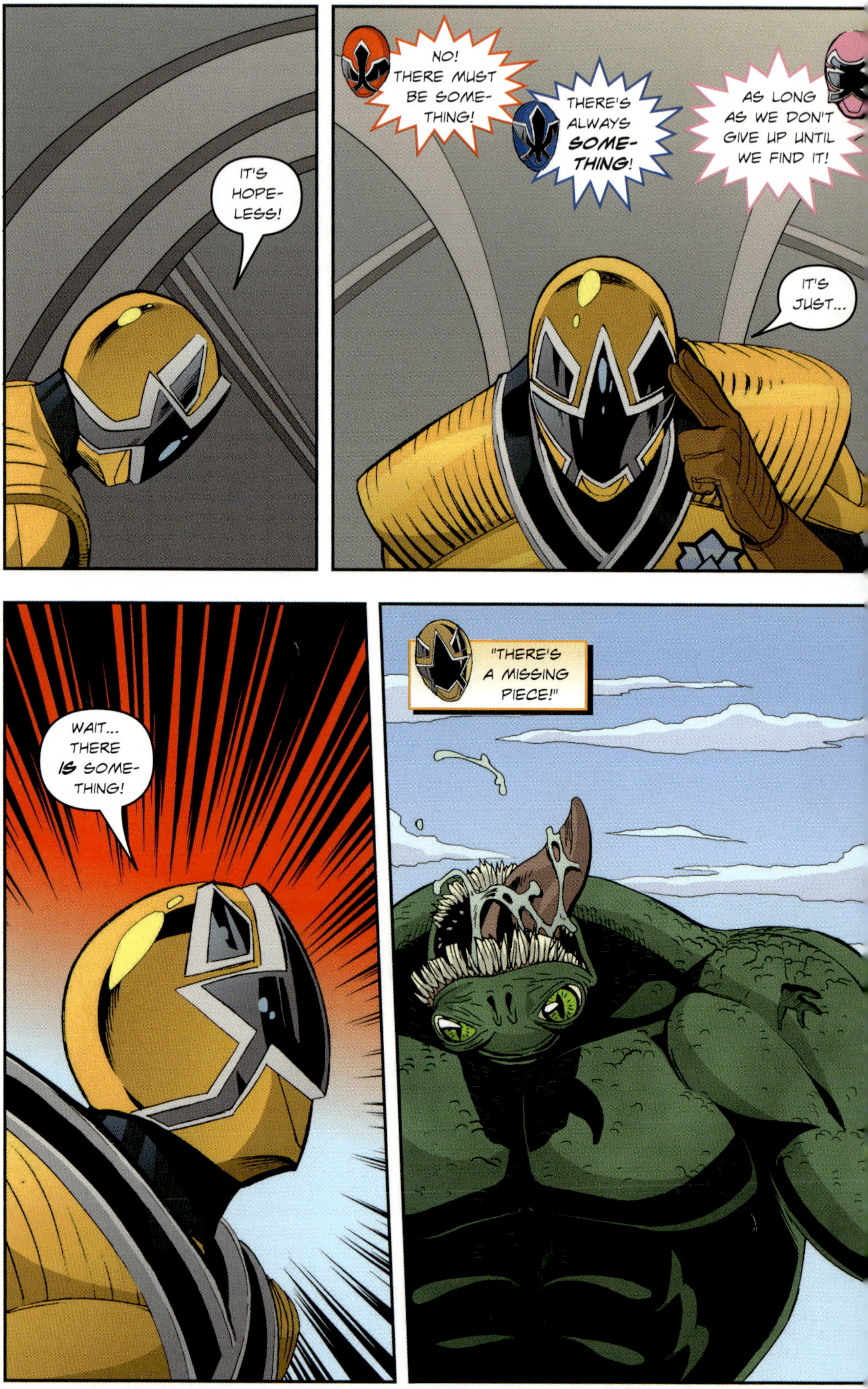
IT'S HOPE-LESS!
NO! THERE MUST BE SOME-THING!
THERE'S ALWAYS SOME-THING!
AS LONG AS WE DON'T GIVE UP UNTIL WE FIND IT!
IT'S JUST...
WAIT... THERE IS SOME-THING!
"THERE'S A MISSING PIECE!"

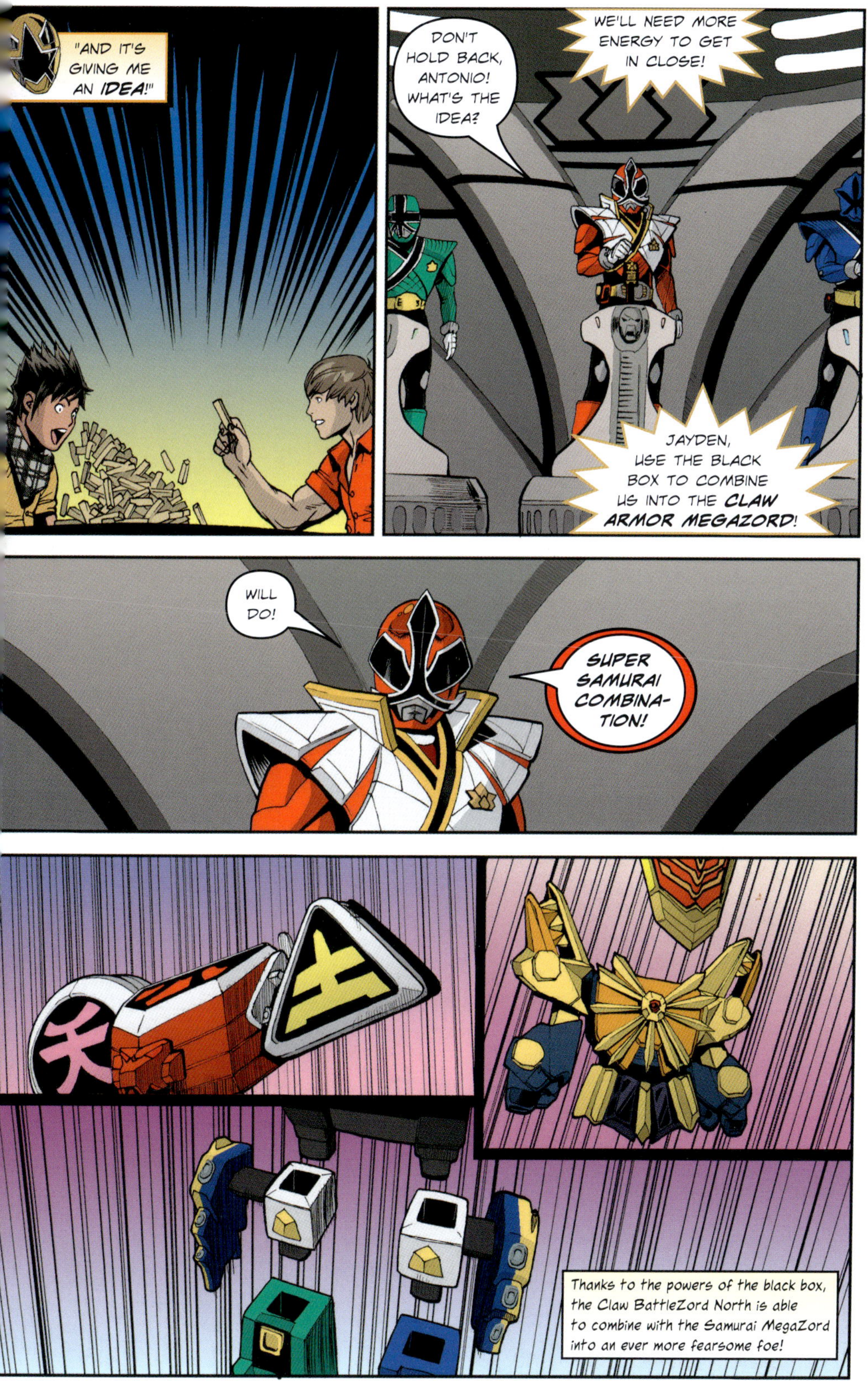
"AND IT'S GIVING ME AN IDEA!"
DON'T HOLD BACK, ANTONIO! WHAT'S THE IDEA?
WE'LL NEED MORE ENERGY TO GET IN CLOSE!
JAYDEN, USE THE BLACK BOX TO COMBINE US INTO THE CLAW ARMOR MEGAZORD!
WILL DO!
SUPER SAMURAI COMBINA-TION!
Thanks to the powers of the black box, the Claw BattleZord North is able to combine with the Samurai MegaZord into an ever more fearsome foe!

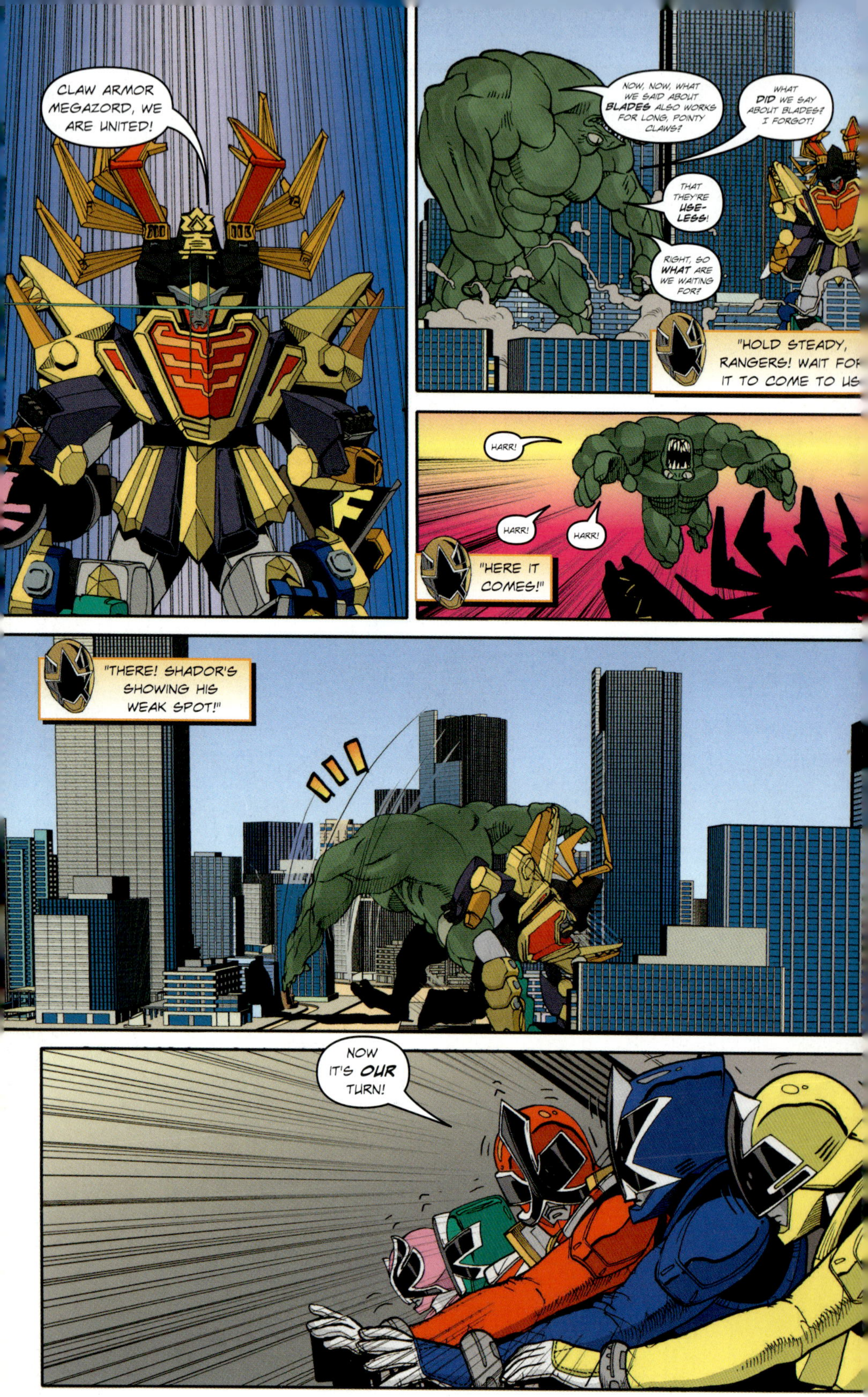
CLAW ARMOR MEGAZORD, WE ARE UNITED!
NOW, NOW, WHAT WE SAID ABOUT BLADES ALSO WORKS FOR LONG, POINTY CLAWS?
WHAT DID WE SAY ABOUT BLADES? I FORGOT!
THAT THEY'RE USE-LESS!
RIGHT, SO WHAT ARE WE WAITING FOR?
"HOLD STEADY, RANGERS! WAIT FOR IT TO COME TO US
HARR!
HARR!
HARR!
"HERE IT COMES!"
"THERE! SHADOR'S SHOWING HIS WEAK SPOT!"
NOW IT'S OUR TURN!

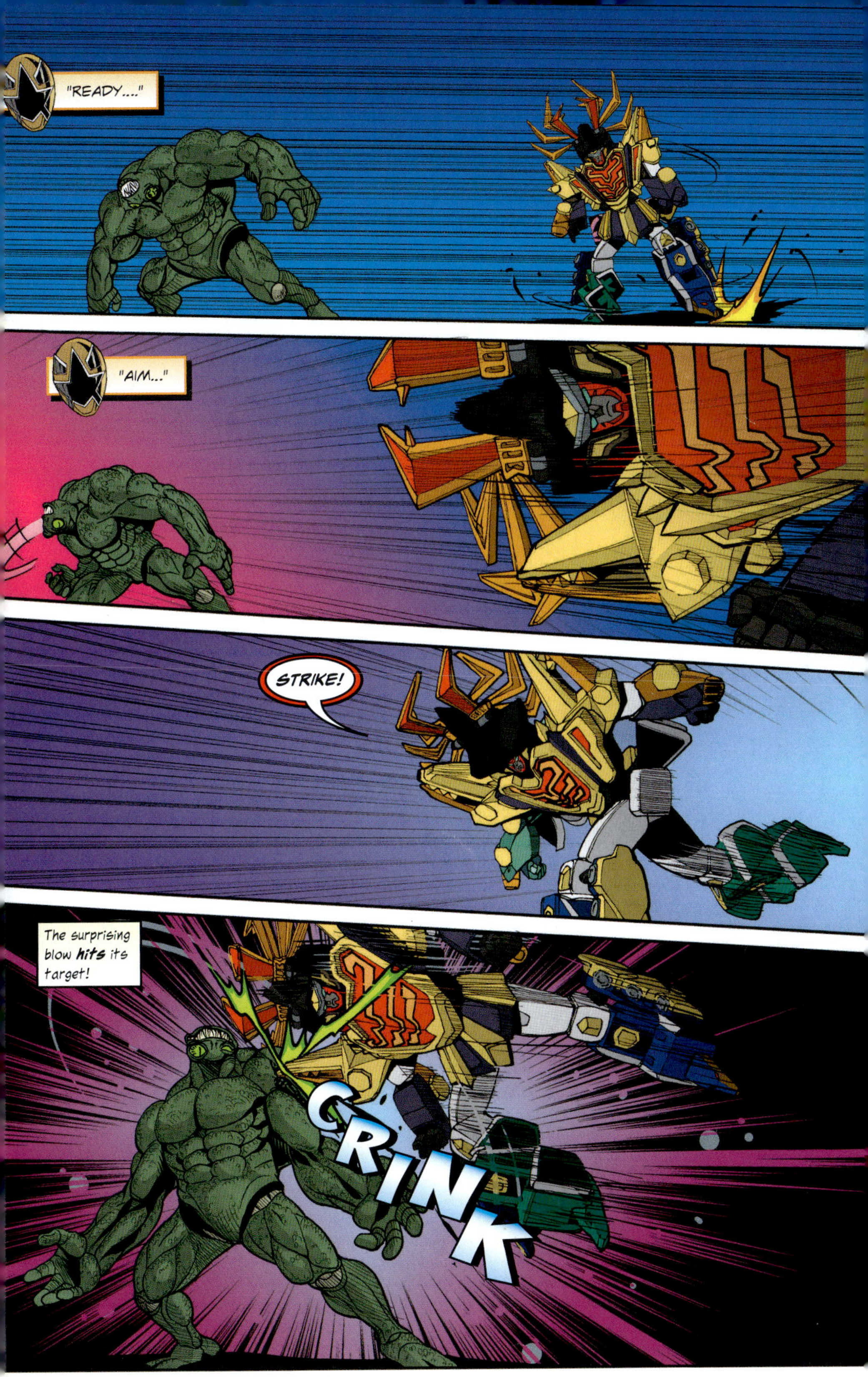
"READY...."
"AIM..."
STRIKE!
The surprising blow hits its target!
CRINK

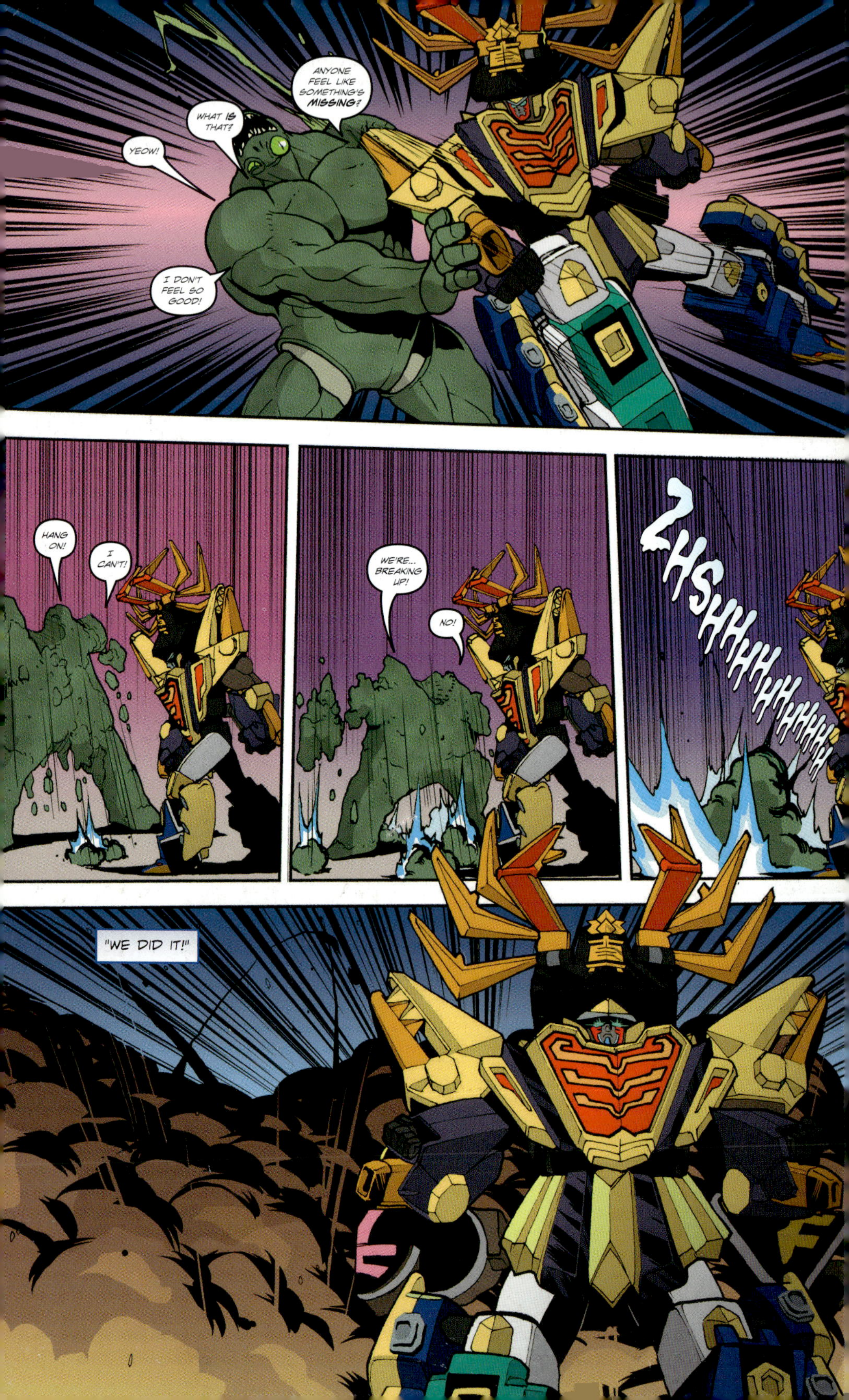
ANYONE FEEL LIKE SOMETHING'S MISSING?
WHAT IS THAT?
YEOW!
I DON'T FEEL SO GOOD!
HANG ON!
I CAN'T!
WE'RE... BREAKING UP!
NO!
ZHSHHHHHHHHHHHH
"WE DID IT!"

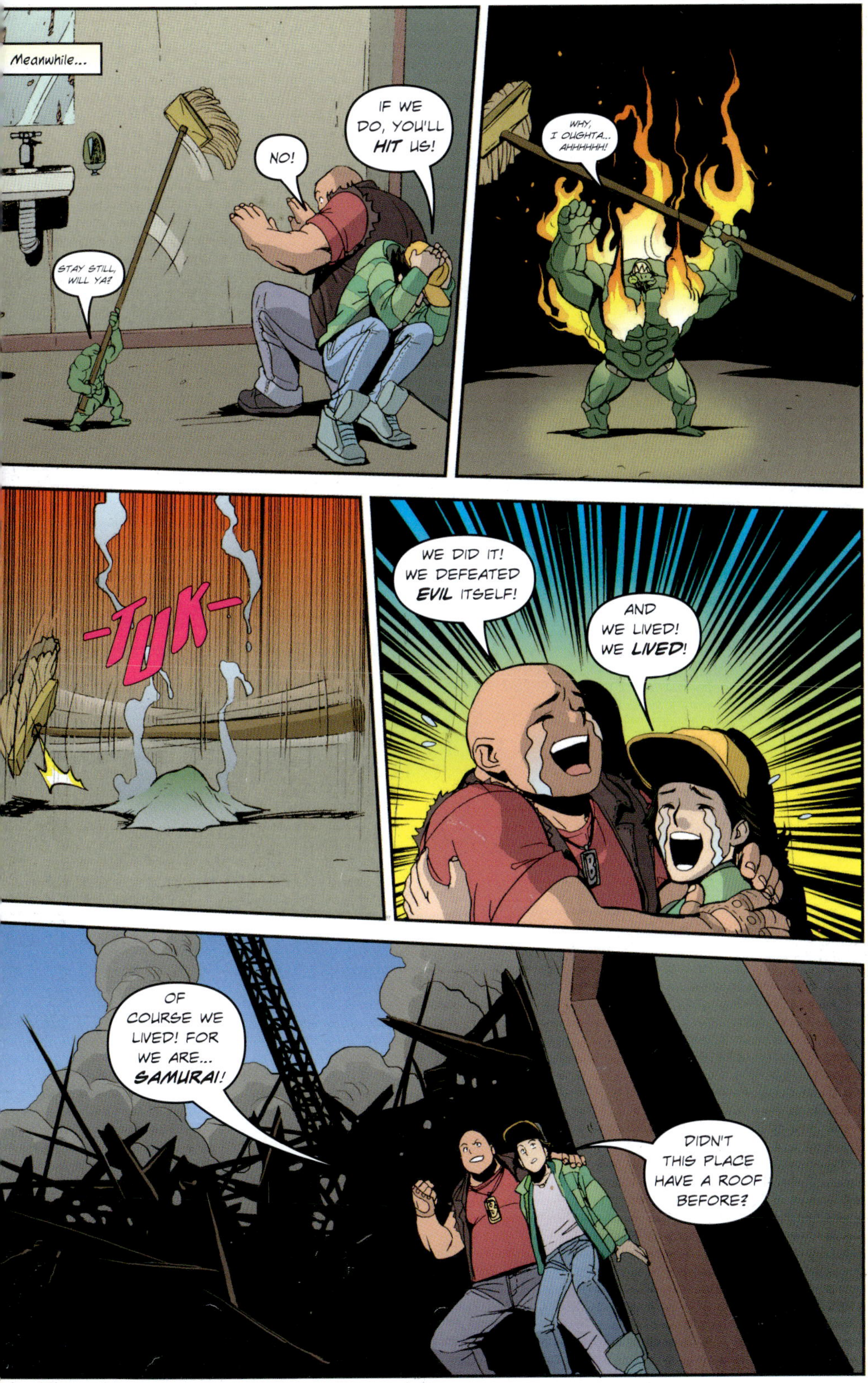
Meanwhile...
STAY STILL, WILL YA?
NO!
IF WE DO, YOU'LL HIT US!
WHY, I OUGHTA... AHHHHHH!
-TUK-
WE DID IT! WE DEFEATED EVIL ITSELF!
AND WE LIVED! WE LIVED!
OF COURSE WE LIVED! FOR WE ARE... SAMURAI!
DIDN'T THIS PLACE HAVE A ROOF BEFORE?

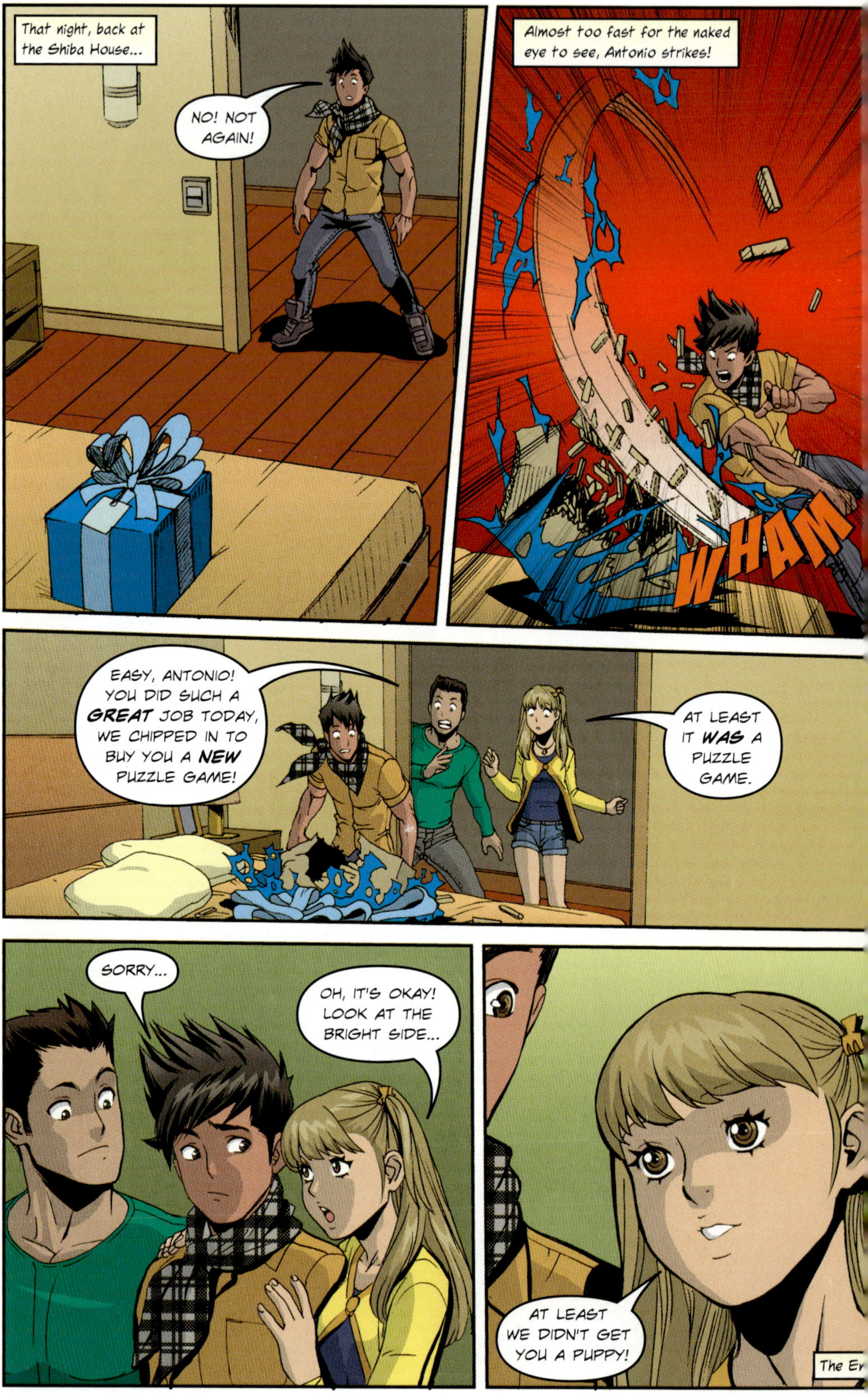
That night, back at the Shiba House...
NO! NOT AGAIN!
Almost too fast for the naked eye to see, Antonio strikes!
WHAM
EASY, ANTONIO! YOU DID SUCH A GREAT JOB TODAY, WE CHIPPED IN TO BUY YOU A NEW PUZZLE GAME!
AT LEAST IT WAS A PUZZLE GAME.
SORRY...
OH, IT'S OKAY! LOOK AT THE BRIGHT SIDE...
AT LEAST WE DIDN'T GET YOU A PUPPY!

WATCH OUT FOR PAPERCUTZ

Editor-in-Chief Jim Salicrup is ready to go into action with the POWER RANGERS at the San Diego Comic-Con!

Welcome to the smashing second SABAN'S POWER RANGERS SUPER SAMURAI graphic novel series from Papercutz. I'm Jim Salicrup, the bleary-eyed EditorZord-in-Chief of Papercutz, the folks dedicated to creating great graphic novels for all ages. As promised last time, in our premiere POWER RANGERS SUPER SAMURAI graphic novel, here's a short bio of super-star artist Paulo Henrique...

Paulo Henrique

Paulo truly is an amazingly talented artist, and we're all thrilled to be working with him at Papercutz! Born in Sao Paolo, Brazil in 1979, he started his professional career drawing MEGAMAN comics for Brazilian publisher Magnum. Later, Paulo drew MYTH WARRIORS for Top Cow Productions, and illustrated volumes 6-20 of THE HARDY BOYS and volumes 1 and 2 of THE HARDY BOYS: THE NEW CASE FILES for Papercutz. Paulo drew volumes 1 and 2 of LEGO® NINJAGO both of which were runaway hits. When approached to draw the POWER RANGERS series, he said it was a "dream job" for him. He lives in Brazil where he is also a musician, and loves watching THE SIMPSONS.

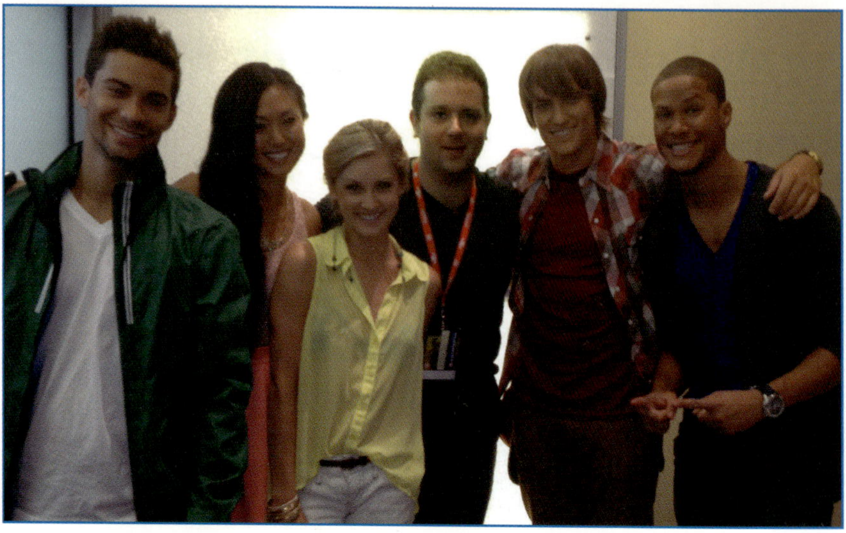

Associate Editor Michael Petranek (third from the right) with the cast of SABAN'S POWER RANGERS SUPER SAMURAI

Recently, Papercutz Associate Editor Michael Petranek attended POWER MORPHICON, a convention just for POWER RANGERS fans, and filed this mini-repor

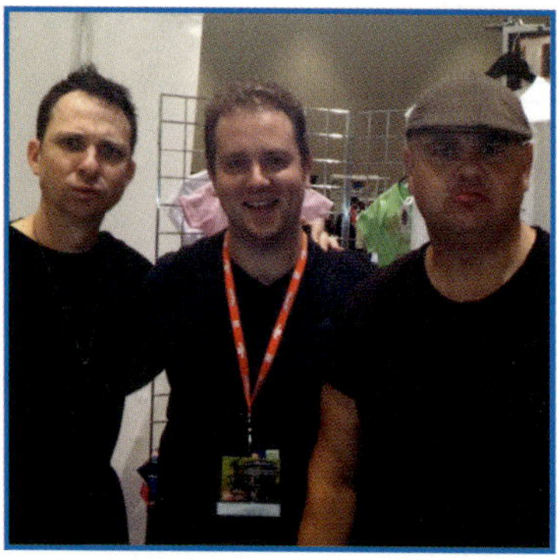

Michael with Jason A. Narvy and Paul Schrier

I had a great time in Pasadena, California attending the third annual Power Morphicon! I brought 1,000 exclusive to-the-show POWER RANGERS mini comics and a few hundred posters, and they were all gone by the first day! I met sever past and current cast members including Jason A. Narvy and Paul Schrier (Skull and Bulk), along wit the cast of POWER RANGERS SUPER SAMURAI. It was a lot of fun to show the actors how Paulo depicts them in the comics, and I found then all to be very warm and friendly. It was very hard keepir a straight face next to Paul – he had me laughing nonstop! The actors enjoyed seeing themselves in comics, and I enjoyed my time with all of them. It was a great show!

I want to thank Umesh Patel at Ranger Crew for introducing me to so many fans, and Saban, without which none of this would have been possible! Thanks to everyone who attended.

As you can tell we're all excited about the POWER RANGERS, and like you, we can' wait till our next POWER RANGERS graphic novel coming soon! Be sure not to miss i

Thanks,

Jim

STAY IN TOUCH!

EMAIL:	papercutz@papercutz.com
WEB:	www.papercutz.com
TWITTER:	@papercutzgn
FACEBOOK:	PAPERCUTZGRAPHICNOVELS
REGULAR MAIL:	Papercutz, 160 Broadway, Suite 700, East Wing, New York, NY 10038

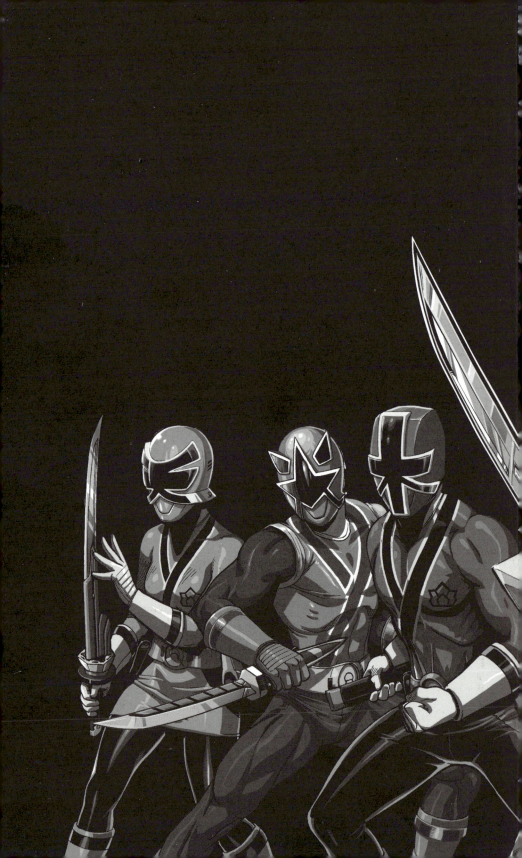